of pure reading pleas...

100 Reasons to Celebrate

We invite you to join us in celebrating
Mills & Boon's centenary. Gerald Mills and
Charles Boon founded Mills & Boon Limited
in 1908 and opened offices in London's Covent
Garden. Since then, Mills & Boon has become
a hallmark for romantic fiction, recognised
around the world.

We're proud of our 100 years of publishing
excellence, which wouldn't have been achieved
without the loyalty and enthusiasm of our
authors and readers.

Thank you!

Each month throughout the year there will
be something new and exciting to mark the
centenary, so watch for your favourite authors,
captivating new stories, special limited
edition collections…and more!

Dear Reader

What a great start to the New Year! Mills & Boon is celebrating its centenary—a hundred years of exciting romance and the joy of compelling love stories to warm our hearts. As a writer and an avid reader of romantic fiction, I'm delighted to be part of, and to be able to share with you, this momentous occasion in Mills and Boon's history.

I think you'll agree with me that the world has changed a great deal in those fabulous years. We have the wonder of technology to make our lives easier and help us to communicate better with one another. The world has been opened up for us through the media of the internet and television. Every day people from across the continents appear on our television screens, and at the touch of a button we can send missives out into cyberspace.

There is a downside to all this, though. What if you later regret what you've sent, or, heaven forbid, you meet up with the object of your scorn?

Television and technology both play a part in bringing together Abby and Matt in my latest book, THE DOCTOR'S LONGED-FOR FAMILY.

Can you imagine the excitement of a TV celebrity coming to a hospital near you? No? Neither can Abby Byford, and she certainly doesn't take kindly to the idea of having a camera crew following her around as she works. As things turn out, though, Matt Calder proves to be far more persistent than she might have imagined.

I've been able to bring Abby and Matt's story to you by being a contributor to this milestone in Mills & Boon's history.

My very best wishes to you all

Joanna

THE DOCTOR'S LONGED-FOR FAMILY

BY
JOANNA NEIL

MILLS & BOON™
Pure reading pleasure

First published in Great Britain 2007
Harlequin Mills & Boon Limited,
Eton House, 18-24 Paradise Road, Richmond, Surrey TW9 1SR

© Joanna Neil 2007

ISBN: 978 0 263 86297 3

Set in Times Roman 10½ on 12 pt
03-0108-51154

Printed and bound in Spain
by Litografia Rosés, S.A., Barcelona

When **Joanna Neil** discovered Mills & Boon®, her life-long addiction to reading crystallised into an exciting new career writing Medical™ Romance. Her characters are probably the outcome of her varied lifestyle, which includes working as a clerk, typist, nurse and infant teacher. She enjoys dressmaking and cooking at her Leicestershire home. Her family includes a husband, son and daughter, an exuberant yellow Labrador and two slightly crazed cockatiels. She currently works with a team of tutors at her local education centre, to provide creative writing workshops for people interested in exploring their own writing ambitions.

Recent titles by the same author:

THE CONSULTANT'S SURPRISE CHILD
EMERGENCY AT RIVERSIDE HOSPITAL
THE LONDON CONSULTANT'S RESCUE
HER VERY SPECIAL CONSULTANT
THE LONDON DOCTOR

CHAPTER ONE

'WELCOME *to Matt Calder's website. You might like to take a look at the guest book area while you're here. There's a message from a Dr Abby Byford, who wants to know why we think it necessary to take the TV cameras along with the ambulance crew when they go out on call.'*

Abby stared at the computer screen, her green eyes widening, her mouth opening in shock. She had imagined that her brief email would have been hidden away somewhere, for his eyes only, or virtually out of sight, or at the very least that it would be lost in an electronic void. She hadn't expected him to reply, or even to use it on his website, yet here was her name, blazoned across the Internet for all to see. He was actually singling her out for attention. Why would he want to do that?

'Is this what passes for entertainment these days? she asks. Why on earth would anyone want to sit and watch injured people having their wounds assessed and then follow them as they go through the process of treatment?'

Abby had been taking bites out of her breakfast toast while she was on the move this morning, but now she let it slide down onto her plate while she stared transfixed at the monitor. Her long, honey-gold hair tumbled down around her face in a wild mass of curls and she swiftly pushed it back out of the way.

'I'm sure many of you will have a view on this, and I'd be glad to see your comments on the website. My own feeling is that we all have a choice in the matter. It's called the channel change button on the remote control, or, if you have the energy, there's always the off switch on the television set.'

Her jaw dropped. That was a total put-down, wasn't it, and what had she done to deserve that kind of treatment? This man, Calder, was impossible. OK, so his television programme had disturbed her, enough to prompt her to send a carefully worded message his way. After all, he had invited comments at the end of the programme, but surely she didn't merit that kind of sarcasm? Hers had been a perfectly legitimate query, but his reply was a pure dig at her expense in front of the thousands who accessed his site.

Her appetite had suddenly disappeared, but it was replaced by a growing rumble of annoyance. She didn't have time for any of this. She was supposed to be getting ready for work, and all she had meant to do was to swiftly check her emails in case any problems had cropped up overnight. Only her friend's message had included a link to the website. 'You have to check this out,' she had written. 'You seem to have stirred something up.'

Now Abby was rapidly regretting the impulse that

had led her to click on the link. Merely thinking about the arrogance of the man brought a red haze to sizzle in front of her eyes. Why had she even bothered to switch on the television the other night? If she had left well alone, she might never have caught sight of his TV show, but she had left it on in the background as she'd dealt with her emails that evening. As she was already online it had been all too easy to let her emotions get away from her and write in to the address given.

They had all been talking about it in A and E, where she worked. 'He has such a wry sense of humour,' Helen, her specialist registrar, had said, 'and when he's on TV he's absolutely brilliant as a presenter. Everybody's watching his show, *Emergency Call.* It's on once a week, in the evening, and he has a weekly slot that deals with different medical topics. It tends to throw up a controversy once in a while. He's interviewed on radio and TV talk shows from time to time, and he writes occasionally, too.'

At least on radio, Abby thought, the listening public wouldn't have been drawn to watch the suffering of the poor young woman who had slipped and fallen down the stairs last night. She was heavily pregnant, and Abby had felt her pain along with her as she had been filmed being carefully transferred into the ambulance.

'It looks as though Megan is going into labour,' Matt Calder had said softly to the camera. 'We'll be by her side through every stage, from here to the delivery room.'

The baby, though, hadn't wanted to wait that long, and soon the presenter had said, 'I don't think we're going to make it to the hospital before this infant is born.'

Remembering, Abby felt her hackles begin to rise all over again. Why was everyone so obsessed with fly-on-the-wall coverage these days?

Her fingers were already stabbing at the keyboard, and she banged out another message to Matt Calder.

'I stand by what I said before,' she wrote. 'Isn't your programme taking things a stretch too far? Do we really need to pry into every aspect of people's lives, even stooping so low as to let cameras intrude on the special, intensely personal moment when a woman gives birth? It's bad enough that the mother's privacy is violated, but doesn't it ever occur to anyone that the infant concerned is being exploited?'

Fuelled by a growing sense of righteousness, she added, 'What depths will be plundered next, I wonder? Will someone be filmed saying, "Oh, I'm sorry, but I really don't feel too well. I think I might not be able to make it through the night, please excuse me while I suck in my last breath. Would you be sure and show the film to my mother? I did so want her to be here with me at the end." How very sad that we have to live our lives through other people.'

Pressing her lips together, she hit the 'send' button and flung her diatribe out into cyberspace. She stood for a moment glaring at the screen, and then she switched off the computer and went to finish getting ready for work.

Her cottage was in a valley at the edge of the Chilterns, and she had a half-hour drive ahead of her to reach the hospital, which was on the outskirts of London. She would need all of that time in order to calm herself down.

It was only when she was sliding into her car a while later that she realised that she had done it again. She had acted without giving herself time to stop and think things through. Had she gone too far? Maybe that sarcasm had been a tad over the top, but something about the show and the website, along with Matt Calder's all too persuasive manner, had managed to ruffle her feathers. Was it possible that she had over-reacted?

Perhaps the truth of the matter was that she was beginning to feel stressed and overworked. Her working life was very different from that of Dr Calder. She had spent long hours the previous day in A and E, doing her best to help the children in her care. She was the doctor in charge of the paediatric emergency department, and it was a responsible job, one that weighed heavily on her at times. She would be the first to admit that it sometimes took its toll on her.

Maybe that was the reason she had responded so badly to the programme. The truth was, Dr Calder, the latest hot new doctor out there enjoying celebrity status, had managed to graze a raw nerve with his bright and breezy invitation to watch events unfold on TV. His role as lead presenter was to comment on events as the trauma team went on its travels attending to casualties. What did he know of hospital targets and patient throughput and the daily anguish of dealing with severely ill patients?

His was a light and fluffy job, involving nothing more than going out and about with the paramedics, or taking part in chat shows on the radio, writing a blog on his website or spouting his own type of wisdom on a variety of health issues. One of them she'd even glanced at briefly, a magazine article on whether or not parents should let their children be vaccinated, and that was a subject guaranteed to put her on edge.

Not that she had seen or heard any of this up until now. She only had Helen's version of what his work entailed and Helen appeared to be heavily biased in his favour.

'He's incredibly good-looking,' she'd enthused. 'Those lovely blue eyes...and his voice... He has such a deep, warm way of talking that he makes me go weak at the knees. He can come and assess my symptoms any day.'

In spite of herself, Abby had laughed. 'You're totally smitten, aren't you?'

Helen had nodded. 'Me and most of the women who work in A and E.'

For her part, Abby hadn't paid much attention to the way he looked. She had only watched the programme in passing as she'd sat at the computer. He had been doing a voice-over some of the time, and mostly her gaze had been riveted to the young woman, Megan, who had been going through the throes of labour. The poor girl had been asking for painkillers, and a film of sweat had broken out on her brow.

Abby had switched off the TV set in a fit of annoyance. Was nothing sacred any more? She had been so fired up by the whole set of events that she had rattled off her comments without a second thought. It was only now, a couple of days later, that she had begun to regret her haste. She was a paediatrician, for heaven's sake, a specialist in A and E, it ought to be beyond her to behave in such an impulsive manner. Why had she even bothered to write in? Hadn't she anything better to do with her time?

And to send off another message at breakfast-time today, well, that had to be pure folly, hadn't it? What on earth was wrong with her?

She pulled out on to the city road and flicked on the car radio so that she wouldn't have to listen to her own thoughts any longer.

'We're glad to have you with us for our twice-weekly programme, *Morning Surgery*, with Dr Matt Calder,' the radio host was saying in reverent tones, and Abby's breath hissed into her lungs. 'Before we open the door to the first patient, we just have time for a few words with our amiable physician.' He paused. 'Dr Calder, I see you've been going through your post in the last few minutes. What's new for today?' Abby's fingers were poised to find the 'off' button, but she had to negotiate traffic and for the moment she let it ride.

'Medical ethics seem to be on the agenda right now,' Dr Calder replied. His voice floated over the airwaves, easygoing, friendly and compellingly smooth, and Abby had no doubt that he would be soothing troubled souls all over the nation.

'People have been replying to the comment made by the doctor who objected to the cameras following patients to the emergency room. I have to say that opinion is divided on the matter, with some for and some against. We've actually had another, rather more strongly worded message from the doctor herself this morning, pointing out that what we're doing is akin to exploitation.'

He proceeded to read out some of her hastily written comments, and Abby's cheeks filled with heat. Having him repeat her words only served to add a new dimension to her embarrassment.

He had stopped to take a breath, and Abby could imagine him giving a wry smile. There was a definite inflection in his voice as he went on, 'I tend to see it more as helping people to learn from others' experiences. We hope that by televising these situations, others might be less afraid and better informed if they should find themselves in similar situations. We are very grateful to Megan and people like her who allow us to share their particular traumas. Some people are extraordinarily outgoing and generous in their outlook. We thank them heartily.'

Some people are extraordinarily outgoing and generous? Abby pressed her lips together. What did that make her? The way he spoke, the implication was that, in contrast, she was clearly a crabby spinster.

By now she had arrived in the grounds of the hospital. She switched off the radio with a jerking twist of her fingers and then she parked the car in her dedicated slot. Sliding out of the driver's seat, she straightened up, locked the doors, and then pulled in a deep breath, assuming the mantle of consultant paediatrician. She had a difficult job to do, and it took every ounce of her reserves. She was the one who set the tone for the A and E department, and people had to be able to trust her to work efficiently and set in place a good atmosphere. Her colleagues relied on her to provide them with guidance and a good example, though what they would make of her recent outbursts via the website they all seemed to favour was anybody's guess.

'I've checked on all the patients in the observation ward,' Helen said, coming to greet her a short time later. 'Everyone seems fairly stable at the moment. I thought maybe you would want to transfer the six-year-old to the children's ward, though. His breathing is still impaired, and he's certainly not well enough to be sent home.'

Abby glanced at the boy's chart. 'Yes, I agree with you. As to the boy with the head injury, we'll need to find him a bed, too. The others will probably be able to go home later today, but we'll monitor them up until lunchtime.'

Helen nodded. 'I'll organise that. We seem to be busy this morning. There's a full waiting room already and we have an incoming patient from a domestic accident, a girl who scalded herself.'

Abby winced. 'It never ends, does it? There's always some poor little scrap who ends up being hurt when it might have been avoided.'

She glanced at Helen. The registrar's black hair was sleek and shining, expertly cut to fall neatly into place at the nape of her neck. It lifted and swirled in a delicate flurry as she turned her head.

'You're looking good today,' Abby remarked. 'Have you been to the hairdresser?'

The registrar grinned. 'I thought I'd better make an effort,' she murmured. 'We have the interviews later today, remember. I figured I should do my best to look impeccably groomed and professional, as you asked me to sit in on them.'

'Is that today?' Abby grimaced. 'I haven't looked at the diary yet but, of course, you're right. I remember thinking that I ought to put in another advertisement. Judging from the response we had, I don't think we're going to find the person we want. Most people want full-time work, but the budget won't run to that. No wonder we're run off our feet most of the time. We need more doctors, not to mention more specialist nurses and a whole load of other staff, like porters and other ancillary staff to take up some of the burden.'

'You never know, we might get lucky. We could find someone who'll be able to do the work of ten men.'

Abby chuckled. 'We can always dream, can't we?'

She went to check on the incoming patient, and for the next couple of hours she was busy dealing with youngsters and their various injuries. She tried, as ever, to push their distress to the back of her mind, and concentrated on providing pain relief and applying treatment that would promote healing and lessen their discomfort.

'We've a child coming in from a traffic accident,' the senior house officer told her. 'It looks like a displaced midshaft femur fracture. He's three years old. Apparently he ran into the road and the car driver didn't manage to stop in time to avoid hitting him.'

'OK, Sam. Make sure that trauma room four is ready to receive him. We'd better have Helen on standby if she's free… and tell radiology to expect him for a CT scan.'

'Will do.' Sam moved away to set things in motion and Abby prepared to take over from the paramedics when they wheeled the little boy into the emergency room.

'He was unconscious when we reached him,' the

paramedic told her. 'An airway's been put in, and we've set up two intravenous lines. His right thigh appears to be deformed from the impact.'

'Thanks for that, Lewis.' She glanced at him. 'I'll let you know how he gets on.'

He looked relieved. 'Thanks, Abby. I'll pop back later on. He's such a tiny little thing. I hope he'll do all right.'

'So do I.'

He moved away and she began to swiftly examine the boy. 'The abdomen is distended, with decreased bowel sounds,' she told Sam when he returned to her side. 'The pelvis is stable, but the thigh is swollen and tense. He's still unresponsive. We'll get a CT of the abdomen to check for any lacerations, and X-ray the leg to see what we're dealing with. It will most likely need fixation, so you should ring for the orthopaedic surgeon to come and take a look.'

'I'm on it.' Sam hurried away once more, while Abby checked with the nurse as to the boy's immediate care.

She was writing out the drugs requisition when a man came over to the trolley and said, 'I think he may have banged his head on the road surface when the accident happened. I'm wondering if he might have a head injury as well as all his other problems.'

Abby glanced up at the man. 'We'll take care of him,' she said. 'We always check for head injury in these cases. Are you the boy's father?'

'No, but his parents are on their way. Apparently he was playing at a friend's house when the accident happened.'

'Oh, I see.' Abby studied him a little more closely. Looking at him was way too distracting, she discovered. He was exceptionally good-looking, with hair that was midnight black, and he was around six feet tall, broad-shouldered and fit, with an athletic build that gave her the idea that he probably worked out regularly. He was wearing an expensively tailored, dark grey suit that sat well on him, and his shirt was a mid-blue, crisp and fresh-looking. She dragged her mind back to the task in hand.

'So who are you?' she asked. 'Are you a relative?'

'No. I was on my way to the hospital when I saw the accident happen, and I stopped to see if I could help in any way. I was concerned about the little fellow, and I just wanted to see how he was doing. I wanted to make sure that you didn't rule out the possibility of a head injury. I think there might be some damage to his spleen as well.'

'You sound very knowledgeable,' Abby remarked as she started to write out the forms for Radiology. 'Are you a doctor?'

'Yes, that's right, I am. I have a strong interest in A and E and the way these departments operate.'

'Well, we'll take care of him. You can rest assured that we'll do everything that's necessary to make certain he's looked after properly,' Abby told him.

She turned back to her small patient, making adjustments to the intravenous infusion she had set up, but after a while she realised that the man was still there, watching her every movement. Why was he so reluctant to leave?

She glanced up at him once more, remembering that he had said he had already been on his way to the hospital when the accident had happened. Her gaze drifted over the clean lines of the suit he was wearing. He certainly wasn't dressed for a casual visit. That, and the fact that he seemed to be taking an interest in what she was doing, appeared to her to add up to one thing. He was probably one of the candidates for the part-time position they had advertised.

'There's no need for you to stay,' she said, 'and I'm sure the little boy's parents will be arriving at any moment. If you're here for the job interview, you could perhaps go and make yourself comfortable in the waiting room. I won't be ready to start on them for a while yet, but I'll ask one of the nurses to show you where you might go and get yourself a cup of coffee in the meantime, if you like. I'll come and find you when I've finished here and let you know how he's doing.'

'Interview?' He gave a slight frown, as though he had forgotten all about it, which wasn't so unlikely, given his morning. Then his expression cleared, and he flicked a glance towards the name badge she was wearing.

He smiled. 'Yes, of course. Thank you, Dr Byford. I think I'll do that. You've been very kind.'

'You're welcome.' She called for a nurse to come and show him the way, and then she turned and gave her attention wholly to the infant, readying him for his CT scan.

'OK, Sam,' she said to the senior house officer. 'You can take Adam along to Radiology now. I'll be in trauma two with the girl with the respiratory infection if you need to find me.'

She didn't give the stranger another thought, except to reflect that he had been unusually persistent. He had waited, and she guessed that he was satisfying himself that all the resuscitation processes were in place so that the child would stand the best chance of recovery.

No one could fault him for that, but wasn't it a little out of place for him to attempt to ingratiate himself with the doctor in charge before any interviews had begun?

Then again, she could have been misjudging him. Her views on men in general had been skewed by the unfortunate events of her past, and it could be that her opinions had been soured.

He seemed to have the child's interests at heart, and she would bear that in mind when next they met.

She glanced at the watch on her wrist. She was already running late. Why was it that in this job the pressure never let up? There was a never-ending stream of poor little souls who needed patching up, and she did her best, but sometimes her best just didn't seem enough.

No wonder Matt Calder was able to breeze through life, charming people with his easy words and blithe spirit. What he knew about stress could probably be written on a postage stamp.

CHAPTER TWO

ABBY studied the results of Adam's CT scan on the computer monitor. 'There's a small head injury,' she told Sam, 'but no sign of any swelling or haemorrhage, so that's good news, at least.'

Her senior house officer nodded, an action that caused a lock of brown hair to waft down over his brow. He was a long, lean young man, always keen to learn, and she was glad to have him on her team.

She switched to views of the child's abdomen, and indicated an area that was giving her cause for concern. 'I'm a bit worried about these patches. There's a laceration to the spleen and a slight contusion to the kidney. We'll need to give him supportive treatment for those, as well as for the contusion we saw on the X-ray of his lungs.' She frowned. 'Our biggest problem, though, is the leg fracture. He'll have to go up to Theatre to have the bones realigned and fixed in place.'

'I had a word with the surgeon about that. He's standing by right now.'

'Good. Let's transfer him over there straight away.'

'I will. I'd like to stay with him, if I may, in case there

are any complications. I could take him to observation as soon as Mr Bradley releases him from the recovery ward.'

'That's fine—as long as there's nothing pressing to keep you down here?' She sent him a questioning glance.

Sam gave that some thought. 'There's only one child that I'm worried about—a two-year-old who was brought in earlier on. She's feverish and very unwell, showing symptoms of infection, but I've ordered lab tests and I'm waiting on the results. I've given her broad-spectrum antibiotics until we have something more specific to go on.'

'It sounds as though you have everything in hand, and of course the nurse will page you if there's a problem. In the meantime, I'll arrange for Adam to be admitted. Let's just hope that we have a bed free. I don't think he's in any condition to be moved to another hospital.'

Sam gave a wry smile. 'I dare say you'll be able to sweet-talk the ward sisters into finding something. You always seem to manage to get around the system when it's really important.'

'Maybe. We'll see.' Sweet-talking didn't always work, and above all it was time-consuming. Time was yet another major resource she was short on these days, although staffing had to be her biggest headache.

She sucked in a breath at the reminder of what she had to do next. The interviews—she was going to have to get a move on, or her goose was well and truly cooked. Would the man who had come in earlier with three-year-old Adam still be waiting around?

She handed over to her second in command, and then paged Helen to let her know that she would be ready to see the candidates in twenty minutes or so. Taking a few moments to grab a coffee in the doctors' lounge, she ran a brush through her hair and tried to tame the mass of wild corkscrew curls. It was a waste of time. No sooner had she put the brush down than her hair spiralled out of control once more, and she had to resort to placing a few clips in strategic places.

She gazed at her reflection in the mirror. Her green eyes stared back at her, shimmering like emeralds, and her lips were a delicate shade of pink, full and pleasantly shaped. She made a faint grimace. At least she didn't look as bad as she felt. There was an element of battle-readiness in the warm flush of her cheeks, and perhaps that was the key to whatever it was that kept her going through thick and thin. She would not give up. She would not cave in when all around her chaos reigned.

The man was not in the waiting room when she went in search of him a short time later. Abby frowned, two small lines indenting her brow. She didn't want to admit to herself that she was disappointed not to find him there, but instinct had somehow nudged her into thinking that he had more staying power than that.

Obviously, she couldn't rely on her instincts any more. They had certainly let her down where Craig had been concerned, hadn't they? He had deceived her into thinking he cared for her, but now her ex-boyfriend was history and a couple of years had passed since she had learned the error of her ways. Her judgement of men was definitely awry.

'Were you looking for me?'

Even coming out of nowhere like that, the voice was instantly recognisable. In fact, there was something oddly familiar about it, considering that she had only met the man that morning.

She turned away from the waiting-room door and looked up at the impeccably dressed doctor. 'Oh, there you are. I wondered if you had given up on me and gone home.'

He shook his head. 'I wouldn't do that. I was hoping that I would be able to talk to you again.'

His glance flickered over her, taking in the soft fabric of her top where it gently caressed the swell of her breasts, and then paused to linger on the smooth line of the skirt where it faithfully followed the curve of her hips. His gaze slid down over the shapeliness of her legs.

His glance lifted, capturing hers before taking a brief detour over the golden cascade of her hair. She felt a rush of heat fill her cheeks under that lazy scrutiny, but she could hardly object as she had been giving him much the same treatment earlier.

'I could see that you were busy,' he murmured, 'and I took the opportunity to follow up on a couple of contacts while I was waiting for you.'

She had no idea what he meant by that, but she said evenly, 'Perhaps we should go into my office? It's just along the corridor.' She was a touch early perhaps, but Helen would be along shortly.

'That sounds like a good idea.' He gave a half-smile and fell into step beside her as she began to walk in the direction she had indicated. 'How is the boy—Adam?'

'He's undergoing surgery at the moment to fix the fractured femur. None of his other injuries appears to be life-threatening, so I'm hoping that he'll be on the mend and ready to leave hospital in two or three weeks.' She pushed open the door to her office and ushered him inside.

'That's good news. I'm glad to hear it.' He stood to one side and closed the door behind her, giving her a smile, and it was as though sunlight had suddenly filled the room. She stood very still for a moment or two. The breath caught in her throat and she had to quell a sudden leap of her senses that threatened to overwhelm her.

It was very odd. This man was a total stranger to her, and her reaction to him was way overboard. She couldn't imagine why she responded to his presence this way, but it must have something vaguely to do with her hormones, she guessed. They must be acting up, that was the answer.

'So you think you might like to work here on a part-time basis?' she murmured, indicating a chair where he could make himself comfortable. 'Would you like to run through your CV for me while I hunt out your file?'

She began to search through the paperwork on her desk. There were four candidates for interview, and it occurred to her that she didn't know which of them he was.

'I don't think I asked your name,' she said, glancing across the table at him.

He hadn't taken up the offer of a seat, but instead was looking around the room with interest, fingering the window-blind so that he could take a look at the view out onto the landscaped hospital grounds.

'No, you didn't,' he murmured, letting the slats of the blind drop back into place. 'Actually, I'm not here about the job at all. I was on my way to keep an appointment with the hospital chief when the accident happened. I was in the car behind the one that hit Adam and, as I said before, I stopped to see if there was anything I could do for him. I called for the ambulance and waited with him until the paramedics came along, and then I used their equipment to intubate him as he had slipped into unconsciousness. As soon as I could see that he was safely inside the ambulance, I followed him here.'

Abby stared at him. 'Oh, I see.' He had stopped to help the child and do what he could for him, and that was good to hear. Somehow it didn't surprise her that he would act in that way. 'Your intervention right from the start probably did more than anything to give him a better chance of recovery.'

Even so, she was a bit nonplussed about her mistake. She felt more than a little foolish now that he had explained what he was doing there, and she said flatly, 'Did you manage to keep your appointment?'

He nodded. 'One of them, at least. I still have to meet up with someone from Administration in half an hour or so.'

She blinked. 'Oh.' It occurred to her that she was beginning to sound repetitive, and she pulled herself together and sent him a puzzled glance. She said cautiously, 'I can't help feeling that I know you from somewhere. Your voice is familiar somehow, but I'm almost certain that we haven't met.'

His mouth made a crooked shape. 'Only through correspondence perhaps. I'm Matt Calder.' He gave her a look from under half closed eyes. 'From the TV programme *Emergency Call*. You are the same, "Abby Byford from the Chilterns", who sent in the email about the show, aren't you? Do you remember me now?'

She gave a sharp intake of breath. Her mouth dropped open and she quickly clamped it shut again. She stared at him in horror. 'You,' she said at last. 'It's you, of all people?'

She shook her head. This was the man who had splattered her email all over his website and read out her comments over the airwaves, and she had actually been civil to him. 'I can't believe this is happening,' she muttered. It felt for all the world as though she had invited the devil himself into her office.

He must have picked up on something of her train of thought because he said in a dry tone, 'I realise that it must have come as a shock to you to find me here, but I can assure you that I'm a perfectly reasonable man. We may have conflicting views, but there's nothing wrong with airing both sides of the argument, is there?'

She didn't answer him right away. Instead, she stood up and started to pace the room, more to work off her rising sense of irritation than anything else. 'You ridiculed me,' she said at last. 'You talked about using the off switch as though I was a moron. I have to tell you, I just don't believe that's the answer. The problem goes much deeper than that. Your programme is an intrusion. You invade people's privacy.' She used the words as though they were weapons, stabbing at him.

He tipped his head slightly to one side, studying her as though she was an interesting specimen. 'I don't believe that's so, and I wasn't implying for an instant that you were lacking intelligence in any sense. I just feel that you can't go on living in a time warp. This type of show is a regular on the media these days.'

Her eyes narrowed. 'Then I have to say I think that's a great pity.'

He frowned, but he wasn't about to let up. 'As far as I'm concerned, it would seem logical to switch off the TV set if you're not happy with what is being shown. I happen to think that what we do is important. We keep people informed about what might happen in certain situations. We show them how the system works and help them to know what to do in an emergency. Knowledge is power after all, and you have to remember that the individuals we film have all given their consent for the footage to be shown on TV.'

Had they really? Abby sniffed in disagreement, a wave of exasperation rising up in her at his bland reply.

'Have they?' She scowled at him. 'And how informed was that poor woman's consent while she was struggling to cope with her labour? From what I could see, she was more concerned that someone would give her painkillers than what was going on all around her.'

'You know, these programmes don't go out live on air, and if it makes you feel better, I can assure you that I made certain that we had Megan's full consent. We asked her again after she'd had the benefit of analgesics and time to think it through. I feel that we were very discreet in the way we filmed the birth, and I don't think the finished product would upset many people.

Nothing was shown that couldn't be watched on day-time television.'

'That's a matter of opinion, though I'll grant that some attempt was made to preserve her dignity. That's something at least, I suppose.' It was a concession of sorts, but she had to drag it up from deep within her. By now she'd definitely had her fill of Dr Matt Calder. 'It still seems like an intrusion to me.'

She straightened her shoulders and went on, 'I want to thank you again for what you did for the little boy…for Adam. I'm sure his parents will be very grateful to you for that.' She hesitated for a moment, and then added, 'As you're not here for an interview, I hope you'll understand if I say goodbye to you now and show you out. I have four other people to see, and when I'm finished here I have patients to attend to.'

Her green eyes flickered. He, on the other hand, probably had nothing more pressing to do than to keep a late lunch appointment with a TV executive.

He didn't appear to be at all fazed by her dismissal of him. Instead, he reached for her hand, taking it between his palms, and said, 'It's been interesting to meet you, Dr Byford. Perhaps we'll have the chance to chat again later today after my appointment with your admin department. I'd very much like to look in on Adam to see how he is doing after his surgery.'

'I dare say that's a possibility.' Abby couldn't think straight with him holding her hand that way, and she wasn't about to commit herself to anything. With any luck, she would be engrossed in her work by then and well out of reach of this man.

He let her go, and slowly her senses began to settle

down once more. She felt hot all over and her head was filled with cotton-wool clouds that only dissipated once he had taken a step back from her. It was just as well they did, because she had work to do. How was she supposed to conduct interviews with her brain in absent mode?

She saw him out of the room, but as she walked out into the corridor with him, she saw that Helen was hurrying towards them. The registrar stopped in her tracks, looking at him in wonder.

'You're Matt Calder from the TV, aren't you?' she said in an oddly breathless tone. 'I can't tell you how much I enjoy your programme…and your website… and I always try to catch your radio slot whenever it's being aired while I'm driving to work.' She stared at him in open-eyed wonder. 'Are you here for the A and E post? Please, say that you are… I'll be the envy of all my friends if you decide to come and work here.'

Matt smiled at her. 'Actually, no, I'm not. I wish it were otherwise, but I'm really only free for a few mornings a week.'

'That's all right. That'll do fine,' Helen said, a note of eagerness in her voice. 'Whatever you can spare— anything—that would be great by me.' Her eyes were wide with anticipation.

Matt gave a soft laugh. 'I'm glad you think so. I'm sure we would work very well together, given the chance, but, alas, I have other commitments at the moment. I'm filming over the next couple of weeks because we still have to do four more shows to complete the series.'

'Couldn't you do the show from here?' Helen was

clearly getting desperate now, and Abby gave her a sharp nudge with the toe of her shoe.

'What?' Helen reluctantly turned her gaze to Abby.

'I think Dr Calder is going to be too busy to do that,' Abby said in an even tone. 'Besides, we shouldn't delay him any longer. He has an appointment to keep.'

'Oh, dear,' Helen murmured. She turned her gaze back to him. 'Do you really? That's such a shame.'

'I do. Dr Byford is quite right. I have to be somewhere else in a few minutes, but you've certainly given me food for thought and I'll bear your suggestion in mind. Perhaps when my recording of *Emergency Call* comes to an end, I'll have more time to spare.' Matt threw a brief sideways glance in Abby's direction, and she wondered if he was deliberately trying to rile her. 'It's been a pleasure to meet both of you.'

'Believe me, the pleasure was all mine,' Helen said huskily.

Abby tugged on her arm and pulled her into the office as Matt turned away and began to stride down the corridor. 'You've obviously taken leave of your senses,' she hissed. 'What are you on?'

'Pheromones,' Helen replied in a distracted voice. 'Sheer, unadulterated male pheromones and animal magnetism. He has it in droves. He should bottle it. He'd make a fortune.'

Abby made a wry face. 'I think you'd better take a minute to pull yourself together,' she said. 'We have work to do.'

Helen sighed. 'I suppose we do, but I can tell you now, not one of the candidates is going to stand up to what I have in mind, not after that.'

'Then I suggest you come back down to planet Earth, and make it quick,' Abby said briskly. 'We have to do some serious interviewing. I need to find someone who can fit in with the department and take some of the burden off our shoulders.'

'Oh, well, if you put it that way…'

A couple of hours later, Abby had to admit that they were no nearer to solving their problem. 'The trouble is, the hours we're offering people are either too few or too many,' she told Helen. 'Nothing seems to fit in with what the interviewees had in mind, and from our point of view we need someone who has strong paediatric qualifications. I don't think that any of those people would be able to work under pressure. They just don't seem to have the experience.'

'It looks as though another advert will have to go in, then?' Helen queried.

'I guess so. I just wonder if we'll get any more response than we had the first time around.'

They made their way back to A and E, and she went to check on the progress of three-year-old Adam. He had come through everything all right, and it cheered her up that she could say as much to the distraught parents who were at his bedside.

'Would you come and take a look at the girl in room one?' Sam asked a little later. 'She's the two-year-old that I mentioned earlier. I'm beginning to be quite worried about her. She hasn't had her full range of vaccinations because of illness in the past, so until the tests come back, I've no idea what I'm dealing with. She isn't responding to antibiotics, and her fever is raging. Her heart rate is fast, as well as her breathing, and the pulse oximetry reading is very low. Do you think we need to do a lumbar puncture?'

They were already walking towards the treatment room. 'That's a very invasive process,' Abby said. 'Is there any sign of a rash?'

Sam shook his head. 'Not as such, but she appears to be very ill. I'm afraid that she's not responding to treatment, and that she might be going into septic shock. It seems as though there's a systemic inflammatory response.'

Abby looked at the toddler and her heart immediately went out to the child. She was dreadfully ill, unresponsive, and a brief examination left Abby concerned that her circulation was shutting down, despite the resuscitation procedures they had put in place.

The parents were tearful, pleading with her to do something for their baby.

'I know this is difficult for you,' she told them. 'Lucy is very ill, but we're doing everything possible to help her. It looks as though she has a bacterial infection of some sort, possibly a form of pneumonia, and so far it isn't responding to treatment. I'm going to change the antibiotics and add something to assist her circulation. We just have to hang in there and wait for the medicine to take effect.'

Turning to Sam, she said in an undertone, 'We'll add a vasopressor to assist the blood flow, and a steroid to see if that will do something to reduce the inflammation.'

Sam looked anxious, but she said softly, 'You're doing all right. You've done everything possible.'

'I hope it's enough.'

She nodded. It was frightening to see a child looking so ill, and Lucy's desperate condition weighed heavily on her mind as she left the room.

Glancing across the expanse of the department, she caught sight of Matt Calder coming in through the main door, and her first instinct was to walk in the opposite direction. She resisted the impulse. Whatever her feelings towards him, she had a job to do, and she couldn't simply take an escape route and avoid him.

Then she saw that he wasn't alone. He had with him the head of administration, and the two of them were chatting amicably, almost as though they were old friends.

A nurse handed her a chart outlining another patient's progress, and she quickly checked the details on it before adding her signature and handing it back. 'You can reduce the observations to half-hourly,' she told the girl. 'His condition seems to be improving at last.'

'I'll do that.' The nurse hurried away, and Abby headed for the trauma room so that she could examine a child who had just been brought in.

'May we interrupt you for a moment?' the head of administration queried gently.

'Of course.' She gave him a polite smile. She had nothing against the man personally, but his department was forever coming up with new edicts to be followed or targets that had to be met, and not one of them ever made her job any easier. The only way he and his kind would ever understand the constraints she was under would be if he was to try working at the rock face, but that wasn't likely to happen in a month of Sundays.

'I believe you've already met my friend, Matt, here?' His smile was encouraging. Clearly he expected an enthusiastic response.

'Yes, we ran into each other earlier today.' So they were pals, were they? Abby mused.

'Good, good. Then you two already have a head start. Matt's writing an article about what goes on in A and E. You know the sort of thing…the challenges you come up against in your daily work, the kind of cases you see on a regular basis. Perhaps you could help him out? I can't think of a better person to show him around.'

Abby glanced at Matt and forced a smile. 'I don't know about giving you the grand tour. It will be more a case of following me around as I work and getting questions in where you can, I should imagine. I don't have the luxury of free time, but you're welcome to tag along.'

The head of administration looked a trifle disconcerted at that, but Matt responded well enough.

'That would be excellent, thank you. I really don't want to put you out in any way.'

Didn't he? So why did she get the feeling she was being coerced into doing this? Anyway, she wasn't going to spend too much time worrying about it, whatever either of them thought about her manner to them.

The trouble with men in authority, from her experience, was that they expected to have everything work their way, and it didn't matter who they trod on to get to where they wanted to be.

Wasn't that what Craig had done? Her ex-boyfriend

had begged her to help him study for his exams, had picked her brains, and then he had walked all over her to get the promotion she had been after. He had taken their shared research paper, the one she had worked on intensively and had been struggling to perfect for over a year, and he had taken all the credit for it himself, using what had mostly been her work to wow the interview board with his so-called expertise.

'I was on my way to see a patient,' she murmured. 'If you'll excuse me?'

'Of course.' The man from Admin clapped Matt on the back and said brightly, 'I'll leave you in Abby's capable hands.' Then he strolled back the way he had come, taking a leisurely route and pausing to admire the colourful murals along the way.

'I don't know how much help I can be to you,' Abby said to Matt, continuing on her way to the trauma room. 'I would have thought you already have some experience of A and E. We all do a stint there during training, don't we?'

'That's true and, to be honest, I actually specialised in it at one time. What I'm really looking for is your take on things. How you feel about your work, and which cases have an effect on you above all others.' He paused for a moment or two, giving her a thoughtful look. 'I noticed that you seemed sad when we walked in here a few minutes ago. Was it because of a difficult problem you had to solve?'

'I don't deal with cases or problems,' she told him. 'I treat sick children.'

She might have expected him to draw back at the snub, but he simply studied her more closely, a glimmer of compassion in his eyes. 'And that's the crux of it, isn't it? That's what makes yours such a heart-rending job.'

She winced at his perception. Why did he have to show that he understood? She didn't like the man, neither did she want to have anything to do with him. He was the enemy, a thorn in her side.

'If you can understand that,' she said, 'then it beggars belief that you should write an article on the pros and cons of vaccination. I have to deal with the fallout from that when parents read your stuff and decide that vaccination isn't for their children. Then I have to try to save the lives of the ones who come in here with meningitis and respiratory infections that overwhelm their immune systems.'

'Did you read the article?'

'Bits of it.' She grimaced. 'Someone had left the magazine open on the table in the doctors' lounge, and I glanced at it in passing.'

He gave a crooked smile. 'I'm not going to win this argument when I'm up against a biased opinion like yours, am I? Perhaps you should have read the article in full before you made up your mind that I'm the devil incarnate.'

'Don't flatter yourself,' she said. 'I tend not to think about you at all.'

That remark might have been a good payback for the putdown he had made on his website, but it didn't have anything near the effect she'd wished for. He simply tilted back his head and laughed.

CHAPTER THREE

'How is the article coming along?' Abby queried, glancing at Matt as he walked up to the reception desk in A and E. He was beautifully turned out, as usual, wearing an immaculate grey suit, with a shirt that was a soft shade of blue. It matched the colour of his eyes, she noted irrelevantly. She watched him take his notepad from his briefcase.

'I'm getting there,' he murmured. 'This last session should see me through to completing it. I already have a wealth of material to write up.'

'That's good.' She frowned, glancing at him through narrowed eyes. Perhaps it would mean that he would soon be gone from under her feet. It was some three weeks since he had arranged to follow her progress through A and E, but at least she had managed to limit his visits to one day a week. She was still uneasy at having him shadow her every move. His presence in the unit put her on edge, though she was hard put to say why.

'I hope you'll be sure to let me see the finished article before it goes to print,' she said on a warning note. Heaven forbid he should take the opportunity to aim a few more swipes at her through his website or, in this case, a Sunday newspaper magazine.

'I will, of course.' His mouth made a crooked slant, one that she was beginning to recognise. He knew exactly what she was thinking, and the fact that he had the ability to read her mind so easily was making her increasingly uncomfortable.

She started towards one of the treatment rooms. 'I'm going to check up on a six-year-old who was brought in here a little earlier. His mother was brought to A and E after a violent domestic incident involving her husband, and the episode seems to have triggered the child's asthma. He's in a bad way.'

Matt frowned. 'Was it simply stress that started the attack, or do you think there could be an underlying infection that's adding to his troubles?'

'There may well be an infection of some sort. He's certainly very chesty. We're doing tests to check on that, and we have him on antibiotic therapy in the meantime, but I think whatever happened at home tipped him over the edge and sent his lungs into spasm.'

They went into the room together a moment later. The little boy was propped up against pillows, and a nurse was checking the monitors and recording his vital signs on a chart.

Abby went over to him and adjusted the oxygen mask, which had become slightly dislodged. 'Breathe in through here for me, Ryan, will you? It will help you to feel better. Here, you can hold it, if you like.'

Ryan struggled to pull in a few breaths of oxygen. He was a frail, thin little boy, with fair hair that added to his pallor. He was ashen-faced and very distressed, so that Abby was worried for him.

He gazed up at her. 'I want my mum…' he said in a thready voice. He turned his head and tried to look around the room, obviously searching for her, but he was very weak and the effort exhausted him. He sank back against the pillows, a teardrop trickling down his cheek.

Abby wished that she could comfort him. She wanted to reach out and hug him. 'I'm sure she'll be here to see you in a little while. We just need to make sure that you're feeling better so that you'll be able to talk to her when she comes to sit with you.'

'My mum's poorly,' the boy said heavily, pulling the mask away from his mouth for an instant, and Abby held it for him so that he could still breathe in the oxygen. 'I wanted to stay with her.'

'I know you did,' Abby said. 'She was hurt, wasn't she? But someone's gone over to the grown-ups' A and E to find out how she is. The nurses are looking after her right now, but as soon as she's strong enough we'll see if we can bring her over to you.'

His expression was solemn, as though he was thinking things through. After a moment or two, he said, his voice barely more than a whisper, 'Daddy hit her in the tummy.' His face started to crumple. 'I tried to stop him. I shouted… But he pushed me out of the way… and my mum fell down.'

His breath gave way, and Abby said gently, 'It must have been very upsetting for you to see that.'

Ryan nodded, a very slight movement of his head, and he started to chew at his bottom lip. Abby glanced up at Matt, and saw that he was frowning, his gaze intent on the boy.

'Has this sort of thing happened before?' he asked.

Again, Ryan nodded. Abby said, 'I know this is hard for you, but you should try not to worry too much. It was very clever of you to ring for the ambulance, and your mother must be very proud of you. You did what you could to help her, and now, because of that, you're both being looked after. You did very well.'

The boy didn't look as though he was too sure of that, and Abby guessed that he would go on fretting until he actually saw his mother again. He stared wretchedly into space, and she moved away from the bedside in order to cast a glance over his chart.

Matt was still frowning, and said in an undertone, 'Where was the father while the boy was ringing for the ambulance, do you know?'

Abby shook her head. 'It seems that he left the house, and no one has seen him since. The paramedics spoke to the neighbours and they said this kind of event wasn't unusual. Apparently he likes to have everything his own way and the couple are always arguing.'

'Has anyone checked the woman's medical records to see if there are any other recorded instances of possible abuse?'

She nodded. 'Yes. I had a word with someone in the department, and they were looking into it. She's had rib fractures, apparently, and a few unexplained falls.'

Matt's jaw flexed. 'He needs to be stopped.'

Abby pressed her lips together. 'You're right, of course, but if his wife won't take a positive stand and bring it out into the open, there's very little that we can do to help her. She has to find the courage to make the first move.'

The nurse came to the bedside and tucked a teddy bear against the pillow, sitting him next to Ryan and folding the toy into the crook of his arm. 'I've brought a friend to keep you company,' she told him. 'Teddy's not very happy. I think he wants a cuddle.'

The boy was too weary to respond, but he rested his fingers over the bear's soft belly, patting him gently, and then he breathed in through the mask, making a ragged little sigh.

Abby turned to Matt and said quietly, 'I'm giving him a bronchodilator through the nebuliser, but it isn't working fast enough, so I'm going to see if I can get him to swallow a dose of prednisolone. I don't think we're going to achieve the best results while he's still upset, though.'

'That's probably true. The best thing would be to keep him as calm as possible.'

The nurse brought the medication in a plastic cup and Abby held it to the boy's lips. He pulled a face, but she urged him to drink it, saying softly, 'I know it doesn't taste very nice, but it will help to make you feel better.'

When he had finished, she helped Ryan to put the mask in place once more, and then she handed the cup back to the nurse, asking quietly, 'Is there any news about his mother?'

'They're still treating her in the adult A and E department for possible damage to her pancreas. Andrea is looking after her over there. She said she would let us know what's happening.'

'Thanks, Jane.'

The girl glanced at Ryan, and then turned back to Abby, her mouth drooping a fraction. 'He's obviously very distressed about what happened.'

'That's not surprising. He must have been very frightened, knowing that he was helpless to stop it.'

Abby was silent for a while, thinking about the boy's anguish, and the nurse said softly, 'You said earlier that you saw his mother when she was brought in, didn't you?'

'Yes, I did. I was just coming from the hospital car park when the ambulance drew up. I could see what a state the boy was in, and his poor mother looked traumatised. It would have been better if they could have stayed together, perhaps, but the staff were worried that his asthma was worsening, so after a while they sent him over here.'

'I thought you seemed to be deeply affected by what happened to his mother. You were very quiet when you came in here first thing.'

'Was I?'

The girl nodded. 'I hope you don't mind me saying, but I've heard something of what happened to you a couple of years ago. You were hurt in a similar way, weren't you? Are you sure that you're all right? It must have brought back memories.'

'I'm fine, thanks. It's just that any kind of aggressive behaviour is disturbing, and I don't like to think of either of them going back to that situation. What happened to me was just a fluke, a one-off. I was in the wrong place at the wrong time, so to speak.'

She sent a quick glance in the boy's direction and

was glad to see that he had closed his eyes and appeared to be resting now. It was awful to think of him living in that tense atmosphere, day after day.

She was startled to realise that the nurse had picked up on her own inner fragility, because she always prided herself on keeping any vulnerability well hidden. She couldn't guard her reactions all the time, though, and nothing had been going the way it should lately. It seemed to her that ever since Matt had come into her life, life had been like a roller-coaster and she was struggling to keep herself from going off the rails.

As to today's events, Abby had never suffered from domestic violence as such, but she didn't want to dwell on exactly what it was that had governed her response to what had happened. It was something she tried to bury deep inside her, but no matter how she tried to prevent it every now and again it would bubble to the surface.

She was uncomfortably aware that Matt was looking on while they were talking. Jane kept her voice low, but he never seemed to miss anything, and she couldn't be sure that he hadn't overheard their conversation. She definitely didn't want him to start asking questions.

She glanced at him, but just at that moment the door opened and Andrea came in, pushing the child's mother in a wheelchair, which she carefully manoeuvred into position beside the boy's bed.

Ryan's mother was a slip of a girl, with long, straw-coloured hair that tumbled across her face, and Abby wondered if she let it stay that way so that it would hide her unhappy expression.

'Melanie,' Abby greeted the woman she had spoken

to briefly earlier in an effort to reassure her that they were going to take good care of her son, 'it's good to see you again. How are you feeling?'

'I'm not too bad.' Her drawn features belied the words, but Abby didn't pursue the matter, because it was clear that Mrs Stanton only had eyes for her little boy. 'How is he?' she asked in a low, anxious tone, gazing at the boy as he lay there unmoving, his eyes closed. She dragged her glance back to Abby.

'He's still very poorly, but his breathing seems to be improving,' Abby said. 'I think the new medication must be taking effect.' She glanced at the nurse beside Melanie. 'Thanks for bringing her to us, Andrea.'

'You're welcome.' The nurse smiled and took a quick, compassionate look at the boy before she gave her attention to the woman once more. 'You take care, Melanie,' she said. 'Remember, you don't have to put up with the situation at home. You can take control of your life, and you can make sure that Ryan doesn't have to go through any of that upset ever again. There are people who will help you.'

'I don't know about that…' Melanie's lips were quivering and she clamped them together to keep them still. 'But thank you, anyway.'

The nurse left the room, and Matt moved to stand alongside the wheelchair. 'Hello, Melanie,' he said quietly. 'I'm Dr Calder. I was sorry to hear about what happened to you. It must have been very upsetting.'

'Yes, it was.' She studied him, her gaze bleak, her expression full of defeat, but something flickered briefly in her eyes. 'I know you, don't I? Aren't you the doctor from the television?' The fact that she recognised him didn't seem to do anything to lift her spirits, and her tone stayed flat.

'That's right, I am.' Matt was very gentle with her, bending down beside the wheelchair and coaxing her to talk to him. 'What did the doctors say to you in A and E? I can see that you have a drainage tube in place, so they've obviously been looking after you.'

He was very perceptive, Abby thought. The tube was mostly covered by the folds of a blanket, so that it was barely discernible, and the receptacle was strapped to the wheelchair for safety.

'Have they managed to sort out all your problems?' he asked. 'Well, the medical ones, at least.'

'I think so. The doctor said he thought my pancreas was damaged slightly and that there was a build-up of blood in my abdomen. They've put a tube in to drain it, and they say it should heal well enough, as long as I rest up for a couple of weeks.'

'Are you going to be able to do that?'

The woman lowered her head and her voice faded into the covering blanket. 'I don't know.'

'Do you have any family who can help you through the next month or so?'

Melanie shook her head.

Matt studied her thoughtfully. 'It's important that you realise you have alternatives. You don't have to stay at home and put up with bad treatment, you know.'

Melanie winced. 'I've nowhere to go, and if I was to try to leave, my husband would come after me.' Her voice wavered. 'Anyway, I'm more worried about Ryan. He looked so ill. He was so upset and frightened.'

'He'll go on feeling that way unless you do something to change the situation. I know it's hard, but you don't have to do it on your own.'

The little boy opened his eyes and blinked slowly. 'Mummy,' he said, a smile creeping over his lips. 'Are you better now?'

'Very nearly,' his mother said. Her face lit up as she looked at her small son, and her features softened. She laid a hand on his head and tenderly stroked his hair. 'How are you feeling, sweetheart? I was so worried about you.'

'I'm all right.' The words came out as a whisper.

He wasn't by any means all right, Abby thought, and neither was his mother. They were traumatised, hurting and exhausted after what they had been through.

'Is Daddy going to come here?' Ryan asked. His eyes were troubled.

'I don't know, Ryan.'

Abby studied the child for a moment or two. Was there any way she could bring this whole situation out into the open so that they could deal with it once and for all? They didn't seem to be getting anywhere very fast. The nurse from the adult A and E unit had tried, and Matt had done what he could to coax Melanie into accepting help, too. The woman had resisted, but Abby had to respect him for trying.

She said carefully, 'How would you feel about it if your daddy were to come here, Ryan?'

The boy didn't answer. Instead, he looked down at the sheet that covered him, and his bottom lip started to quiver.

Matt was looking at Melanie, and now he said quietly, 'I know of some agencies that can look after both of you. They can keep you safe and advise you on how to get through any difficulties.'

Melanie didn't give any sign that she believed that, and instead, as she glanced towards the door, she bit her lip, as though she had the worries of the world on her shoulders. She tensed suddenly, staring through the partitioning glass wall, and her shoulders stiffened as though she was bracing herself.

Abby could see what was troubling her when the door opened and a man walked into the room. He was smartly dressed, wearing a dark suit and a crisp, pale-coloured shirt.

'So there you are,' he said, his gaze homing in on Melanie and ignoring everyone else. 'I've been worried sick about you. They told me you were hurt and that you had been brought here. I know you had another of your falls, but you were fine when I left the house. You just need to rest up.' He frowned. 'I was only away for half an hour, and you disappeared. I've been looking everywhere for you.'

His glance went to the bed. 'What's Ryan doing here?'

'He had an asthma attack.' Melanie's voice was barely audible, and she seemed to shrink into herself. Abby's gaze caught the faint tremor that affected her hand.

'Another one? It's time he grew out of those. You both need to be at home where I can look after you.' He swivelled around and glanced dismissively at Matt and Abby. 'Let's get that organised right now.'

Abby intervened when he would have taken hold of the wheelchair. 'Mr Stanton?' she queried.

He nodded briefly. 'Who are you?'

'I'm Dr Byford. I'm looking after Ryan. I'm afraid neither he nor your wife are in any condition to go anywhere. Ryan needs to be monitored constantly because his oxygen level is dangerously low, and your wife has just undergone minor surgery. We have to keep an eye on her in case any complications arise.'

'Surgery? They told me over in A and E that she was bruised where she fell onto the arm of the chair. She'll be all right. I can take care of her. You don't know my wife. She hates being in these places. They make her nervous and unsettled. She'll be far better off at home with me.'

'I'm afraid that's not an option, Mr Stanton. You have to understand that it would be dangerous for either of them to be discharged right now. Arrangements have been put in place for them to be admitted.'

'Then you'll have to cancel them.'

She tilted her head back. 'I'm sorry, but that wouldn't be wise.'

His expression hardened. 'I don't think you realise who you're dealing with. I know what's best for my wife and son.'

He took hold of the handles of the wheelchair and started to turn it around. Ryan began to whimper as he saw his mother being trundled away, and as his lungs constricted the oxygen monitor started to bleep a warning. The nurse hurried over to attend to him.

Abby positioned herself in front of the door. 'So do I, Mr Stanton. I'm in charge here, and I have a duty of care to my patients. If you insist on attempting to remove them against their will, I shall have to call Security.'

Her heart was thumping erratically as she said that.

She was taking a chance here because Melanie hadn't actually said anything about wanting to stay, and it was only the woman's haunted expression that drove her on…that and Ryan's distress. She was going out on a limb to defend them both.

The man's jaw hardened, his mouth making an ugly line. 'You think you're going to stop me from taking my family home where they belong? You don't have a leg to stand on.' He swung around to look at his wife. 'Tell her, Mel. You want to come home, don't you?' His mouth was curved as though in a smile, but his eyes were as cold as ice, daring her to oppose him.

'I suppose I…I…'

Abby was desperately afraid that Melanie would give in to his pressure. What on earth could she do to resolve the situation if the woman allowed him to badger her? She had already extended her powers to the limit and beyond.

'Your wife is too ill to make that decision,' Matt intervened, moving to stand between Melanie and her husband, and Abby felt an immediate rush of relief sweep through her. 'Leaving here at this time could lead to her suffering a life-threatening relapse, and if you persist in trying to remove her, I will testify as such in court. The same applies to your son. You can hear the heart monitor bleeping. It means that his heart rate has accelerated dangerously and he is in desperate need of medical attention. Your presence here is hindering the accident and emergency team from being able to do their job. I suggest you leave before I assist Dr Byford in calling Security to remove you.'

Matt spoke in a low voice but with such deadly em-

phasis that no one was in any doubt that he was prepared to stand his ground. He stood a head taller than
the other man, and his shoulders were squared, present-
ing an immovable force, opposition to be reckoned
with.

Abby had the strong impression that, instead of
waiting for Security to arrive, he would remove the
man bodily if he didn't go voluntarily in the next few
seconds.

Mr Stanton must have gained the same idea because
he appeared to be having second thoughts. He let go
of the wheelchair and started to back away.

'I'll go,' he said addressing Abby, 'for the moment,
because I want the best for my wife and son. You had
better take good care of them. If anything happens to
either one of them, I'll lay the blame at your door, you
can be sure of that.'

Abby didn't answer him. She stood to one side and
opened the door so that he could sweep through it
without a backward glance. When he had gone she
closed it again and stood for a moment, breathing in
deeply and letting all her nervous energy dissipate.
Her heart was still pounding.

'Thank you for that,' she said under her breath, a
moment later, glancing up at Matt. 'You have no idea
how relieved I am right now.'

'I can guess,' he said, his mouth making a brief twist.
'That was touch and go for a while there, wasn't it?'

She nodded, and hurried to Ryan's bedside to adjust
his nebuliser. 'Let's give him another dose of the bronchodilator,' she told the nurse. 'It should help to get him
back on track.'

To Ryan, she said softly, 'It's going to be all right, Ryan. We're going to look after you and your mother.'

Ryan's lips moved faintly. 'Thank you,' she thought she heard him say.

Matt, in the meantime, was talking to Melanie. He bent towards her. 'I could arrange for you and Ryan to go to a shelter when you're well enough to leave here,' he said. 'I'll take you there myself, if you like. I know the people who run the place, and I know that they will take good care of you. They're very experienced in these kinds of situations. They'll make arrangements to fetch your belongings from your house, or fix you up with alternatives, and they'll help you to find safe accommodation just as soon as you feel ready. What do you say? Would you like me to set the wheels in motion?'

Melanie nodded. 'Yes, please.' She glanced at her son and then hesitated. 'I can't do it on my own. I'm too scared.'

'You won't have to. I'll sort it all out for you.'

'Thank you.' She gave a long, soft sigh, and then asked quietly, 'Will I have to see him again—my husband? I mean, he'll come back here, won't he? He said he would, and I can't think straight when he's around. I try to say something, but my tongue sticks to my mouth and I can't get the words out.'

'You don't have to see him if you don't want to. We can make sure that he's not allowed to come anywhere near you or your son. You have to start thinking of what's best for you. It's time for you to start taking control of your own life.'

Abby watched him gently coax the woman into

talking to him. He carefully tried to shore up her defences and as she listened to his deep, calm voice Abby felt a ripple of heat start up in the region of her chest and slowly spread throughout her whole body. He was making sure that this woman wouldn't suffer at the hands of that violent man ever again. She knew, without doubt, that he would see this plan through, and that Ryan would have the chance to grow up to be a happy child. She could feel it in her bones.

A smile curved her mouth. Matt began to straighten up and he looked at her across the room at just that moment, as though he had intercepted the warm thoughts that were winging their way towards him.

'They'll be OK,' he said softly.

'Yes. Thank you for that.'

When she was sure that Ryan's breathing had stabilised and that he was comfortable once more, she left him and his mother in the care of the nurse.

Matt followed her out into the main thoroughfare of the A and E department.

'I was really glad to have you on my side then,' she said. 'It was such a relief when you stepped in and stood up to him.'

'I was glad to be able to do something.' Matt gave her a faint smile. 'That's the thing about A and E, isn't it? No day is ever the same.'

'I suppose that's true.' A sudden thought occurred to her and she sent him a penetrating stare. 'I'm warning you, don't you dare repeat anything of what went on in there.' She used a stern tone, but her mouth tilted at the corners, softening the effect, and he nodded acknowledgement.

His expression was wry. 'You don't trust me an inch, do you?'

'Well, perhaps a little bit more than that, after what you did in there,' she murmured. 'You were brilliant, but don't let it go to your head, will you?'

'As if I would ever get the chance,' he retorted, sending her an assessing glance. His blue eyes glimmered momentarily. 'I don't know what it is about you, Abby, but there's something that intrigues me. I can't quite work you out.'

'Then perhaps you should stop trying.' She headed towards the reception desk and began to sift through the patients' files.

He smiled crookedly. 'You know that's not my way.' He watched her as she picked out one of the folders and began to glance through it. 'I thought you handled Stanton very well back there. You were unfailingly polite, but you let him know that you weren't someone to be messed with.'

He let his glance travel over her face, lingering on the determined curve of her mouth and the upward tilt of her jaw. 'I just have this feeling that you have pretty much the same attitude towards men in general, and I'm wondering how that might have come about.'

'I think you're misguided,' she said. 'After all, I get on very well with my male colleagues, and as far as I'm aware they don't appear to have a problem with me.'

'Hmm…maybe that's true, but there's something that doesn't quite add up.' His expression was thoughtful. 'I wonder what kind of personal life you have, if any.'

'The kind that's personal,' she retorted. She wrote

something on the chart and then looked up at him once more. 'I really have to get on,' she said.

'Yes.' He studied her. 'You're a tough nut to crack, Abby, but I expect I'll manage it sooner or later, one way or another. It's just a question of finding out where the fracture line is.'

Her eyes widened. And then her vulnerabilities would be exposed for all to see, wouldn't they?

Abby wasn't about to let that happen, under any circumstances. She had been hurt once before, and now she kept a guard on her feelings with a passionate intensity. Matt was in for a surprise if he really thought she was going to be an easy challenge.

CHAPTER FOUR

ABBY was driving into the hospital car park as the radio news bulletin came to a close. The theme tune for *Morning Surgery* started up, and she blinked in surprise. The man seemed to be with her everywhere she went. Was there no escaping him?

She carefully negotiated her way into her parking slot, and the last notes of music faded away, to be replaced by Matt's deep, honeyed tones. The voice was coming to her over the airwaves, she knew that, but it startled her all the same, because it felt every bit as though he was there in the passenger seat beside her. She suddenly felt warm all over.

'A patient came to see me the other day,' Matt was saying. 'He looked haggard, as though he was washed out. "I don't understand what's wrong with me, Doctor. I'm always so tired these days," he said. "There's so much that I need to do, and I've no energy to do anything. It's beginning to get me down."

'I sympathised with him. "Yes, I know exactly what you mean," I said. "You just want to sleep all day, and you can't be bothered with anything. It's odd, you know, but I feel that way, too. It's horrible, isn't it? I wonder what's causing it?''

Abby laughed, in spite of herself. The man was impossible. It was hard to stay cross with him for too long, because every time she steeled herself for a fight, he disarmed her with his understanding and his calming ways. It was very strange, but he was starting to get to her, and even though she hadn't seen him for a couple of weeks, she found herself thinking about him at odd times of the day and night.

She was almost disappointed that he had finished shadowing her in the department…almost, but not quite. Any empathy she felt towards him had to be a blip, didn't it? She simply hadn't been herself lately had she?

When she switched off the radio a moment or two later, he was advising the listeners about the benefits of a nutritious diet and giving them pointers about how to get a good night's sleep.

His voice was soothing, easy on the ear, and, despite his humorous remarks, he made it seem as though he cared about people and their problems. Part of her wanted to go on listening to him, but time was running on and she quelled the urge to do that and hurried into A and E instead.

'Someone's waiting to see you,' Helen said as she walked into the main thoroughfare of the unit.

'Oh, who's that?'

'Do you remember Adam, the three-year-old boy from the traffic accident a few weeks back?'

'Of course, yes I do.' Abby's eyes widened. 'I'd heard that he was discharged from hospital a fortnight ago. How is he doing, do you know?'

'Go and see for yourself.' Helen was smiling. 'He's in the waiting room with his mother. He was asking for you.'

'Was he? I'd better go and see him, then, before I get started on anything else.' She hurried away, turning into the corridor and walking briskly towards the waiting room. She pushed open the door.

The little boy was in a wheelchair, and his mother was by his side, but they weren't the only people in the room. Matt was there, too, and Abby stood for a moment, absorbing that fact. It took her aback to see him standing there, looking so fit and energetic, so full of vitality and enthusiasm for life.

He was chatting to the young woman, the boy's mother, and she was clearly enjoying the encounter. Why wouldn't she? He had charisma in bucket loads.

As Abby walked into the room, he must have said something to make the little boy smile because Adam said brightly, 'I'm going to do that. Mummy said she'd buy me a new football so that I can practise my kicking when my leg's mended.'

'My word, but you're getting better fast,' Abby said, closing the door behind her and going further into the room. She smiled at the boy and his mother, and then nodded towards Matt.

'I hadn't realised that you would be at the hospital today,' she told him. 'I thought you had finished collecting material for your article.' She frowned. 'Besides, weren't you on the radio just a short while ago? How is it that you're here now?'

'You're right, I was on the radio. The programmes are prerecorded for the most part an hour or so before they go out on air. That gives me time to do other things. As to the article, yes, it's finished. I came here to talk to Admin about something else, and I just happened to run into Adam and his mother.'

'That was fortunate,' Abby commented.

'Yes, it was,' the boy's mother put in. 'I've been wanting to thank him for helping Adam that day. He was there from the moment the accident happened, and I'm so glad that he stopped to take care of him. We wanted to thank you, too, for all that you did for us.'

'It's good to see him on the mend,' Abby said. 'I'm more than glad that I was able to do something for him.'

The three-year-old looked up at Abby and said shyly, 'I bringed you some flowers, cos you was nice to me when I was poorly and you maked me better. You gived me some sweeties when I didn't like the medicine, and you bringed me a jig-saw puzzle when I was grumpy in bed.' He thrust out a posy of sweet-smelling freesias in front of him, and Abby accepted them from him, her lips curving in a smile.

'Thank you, so much, Adam,' she said. 'What a lovely thought. These are so beautiful, and the scent is lovely. These are my very favourite flowers.'

Adam's face lit up with pleasure. 'I choosed them,' he said. 'I thought you might like them.'

'I do, very much. I shall put them in water straight away.' She sent a warm glance towards his mother to show her appreciation, and then she turned to look at the cast on the boy's leg. It was covered with pictures and signatures. 'You've quite a collection there, haven't you? Can I add a picture?'

The child nodded, and she bent down to add a pretty butterfly and a get-well-soon message. He beamed at her and started to examine all the other drawings. 'Matt drawed me a football,' he said. 'There it is, see? That's me, kicking it into the goal.'

'That will remind you what to do when you're up and about again, won't it?' Abby said. She spoke to Adam and his mother for a little while longer, before reluctantly excusing herself. 'I have to go and get on with some work now,' she told Adam, 'but I'm really glad that you came to see me, and I'm so happy that you're feeling better.'

Matt said his goodbyes, too, and they left the room together. They made their way back to the main unit.

'So what is it you're here to see Admin about today?' she asked him as she went into the small kitchen area and filled a vase with water. 'Is it about another article that you're writing?' A sudden thought occurred to her, and she added quickly, 'You're not here to set up a TV programme, are you?'

He lifted a dark brow. 'Actually, that had crossed my mind. From what I've seen so far of what goes on around here, it would make a terrific series.'

She shook her head. 'No, no…believe me, it wouldn't.' She arranged the flowers in the vase and sniffed their delicate perfume. 'This is children's A and E. It's far too harrowing for home viewing, and I really don't think it's a good idea. Besides, it would mean that you would be filming me at some point, and I certainly don't want to be paraded on television like a specimen in a jar for all to see.'

He looked her over. 'You'd make a very nice

specimen,' he said, his mouth tilting slightly. 'You're extremely photogenic, with those classic features and that cascade of dark gold curls. You're beautifully turned out...' His glance made an appreciative tour over her before he continued, 'Very shapely, and easy on the eye.'

Her cheeks heated under his penetrating scrutiny. Did he really think she looked good? 'Well, I don't think it's a very good idea, so please drop it,' she said in a firm tone.

'That would be a great pity,' he murmured. 'It's more than just the way you look. You're good at your job, and you have lots of different vocal attributes to go along with it. We get the whole gamut with you, don't we, from brisk and businesslike to gentle and soothing. I think you'd make for very good TV.'

'I'm afraid I don't agree with you on that.' She drew back her shoulders...brisk and businesslike indeed. Her mouth set in a straight line. 'In any case, I'm far too busy to have cameras following me around. They'll just get in the way, and that will make me cross. You wouldn't want to see me when I'm cross.'

He chuckled. 'I think it's too late for that already. I was there when you first discovered who I really was, remember? You may not have been hopping mad, in the literal sense, but you managed to get your opinion of me and my work across pretty well all the same. Somehow I think cold dismissal can be far more effective than fire and fury.'

She flicked a glance over him. 'I doubt that it had that much effect on you,' she murmured. 'I don't recall that you were put off in any way.' She started on her way out of the kitchen and walked over to the reception desk in the main area of the A and E unit.

He went with her. 'Ah well, I've had a fair amount of experience of dealing with people of all kinds of temperaments. I suppose it goes with the territory—being an emergency doctor helps to prepare you for anything. I think you would find that being so overwhelmed with work as you are usually, you would soon forget that the cameras were around.'

'I doubt that would happen, and I shouldn't think any of the children in my care would be too happy to be filmed either.' She placed the vase on the table. The flowers were colourful and they brightened up the place.

'You'd be surprised. Children are wonderful when it comes to TV. They are so natural, and so inquisitive. It's a delight to work with them.'

'It isn't so delightful when they're poorly. If you're so experienced in emergency work, I would have thought you would know that.'

He nodded. 'I do. But the thing with children is that they're down one minute and up the next. They often recover remarkably well from the horrible things that befall them. Take Adam, for instance. You wouldn't think that he was the same child that was brought in here unconscious not so long ago, and I can well imagine how he would be on camera. He'd be a star.'

'I dare say you're right, but it's still an intrusion.' She picked out a chart from one of the wire trays on the desk. 'How did you get on with Mrs Stanton and Ryan, by the way? I heard that you were making arrangements for them to go and settle in a new place where they would be safe from Ryan's dad. Did everything go off all right?'

'It did. I made sure that they reached the shelter safely, and I gather that they've made friends with some of the other women and children who are staying there. I've put out some feelers to find a more permanent home for them when they're up to moving on at some point in the future.'

'It sounds as though you're planning on keeping in touch with them.'

'I am. For the moment, though, I think Melanie needs breathing space to build up her self-esteem and find her confidence, so that she'll be better able to cope. I know the woman who runs the shelter, and she's very good at helping women to help themselves.'

'I'm glad that Melanie's managing to make a fresh start. It will be good for Ryan's health, too, if he can be free from the worry of wanting to protect his mother.' She studied the chart momentarily and then said, 'I really have to get on and see some patients. We've a full waiting room already, and I dare say before too long we'll have youngsters coming in by ambulance.'

'Unfortunately, you're probably right.' He made to move out of her way and said, 'I need to go and have a word with Admin.'

She watched him walk away and then tried to put all thoughts of him from her mind. That wasn't too difficult to do with an influx of casualties needing her attention, but in the odd moment when there was a lull, she caught herself thinking about him. She especially wanted to know what he was discussing with Admin.

'He's looking into the facts about MRSA in hospitals and how we cope with keeping this place relatively free from dangerous bacteria,' Helen told her. 'I offered to help him with his research, but he said he thought he could manage.' She looked crestfallen about that, and when Abby sent her a wry look, she added, 'Well, can you blame me? He's gorgeous.'

Yes, he was, even Abby had to concede that, but she didn't want to think about it any more than was absolutely necessary. Her nervous system was on the defensive already where he was concerned, and it went against the grain that he should be so much on her mind, because she had told herself that she didn't want anything to do with men. She was better off without them, wasn't she?

Over the course of the day, the pace of activity in the unit was hectic and her mood became decidedly frazzled. If only they could have filled the temporary post, life would be so much easier. As it was, she and her team had been busy dealing with the aftermath of a nasty traffic accident, and then there were several children who presented with difficult to diagnose problems.

Once she had sorted those out, she was hoping that she might be able to take a well-earned break, but it wasn't to be. Sam was struggling with a number of high-priority patients, and had turned to her for help on a number of occasions, and the nurses were asking for her advice on several of the children in their care, as well as having trouble with some of the equipment. Even Helen was debating what she ought to do about a child with an unexplained limp. Right now she was looking after a two-year-old girl who had a high fever. The child was convulsing and the parents were frantic in case she was seriously ill.

Abby went to examine the little girl. 'I think Maisie is having a simple febrile seizure, probably caused by an infection of some sort,' she reassured the parents.

She wrote out the medication chart and handed it to the nurse who was assisting her. 'We'll have to wait for the results of the tests before we can be sure of exactly what's going on. In the meantime we'll give her diazepam to control the seizures and Calpol to bring down her temperature. She may need antibiotics, too, if it turns out that there's a bacterial cause.'

She went from there to help the nurses with their queries and programmed the display on the computerised infuser so that they could interpret the readings it was giving them. Then she went to find out what was wrong with Helen's ten-year-old patient.

'I can't find anything on the X-ray that points to the child's problem,' Helen said, 'and all the tests I've done have come up negative, except for a mild joint effusion that showed up on the ultrasound scan. He doesn't appear to be ill in himself, but he's recovering from an upper respiratory tract infection and now he has a low-grade fever. His hip is giving him a lot of trouble, though, and he has a definite limp.'

Abby examined the boy. 'Have you been doing a lot of sports activity lately, Ben?' she asked him, but he shook his head.

'No. I didn't feel like it. I was supposed to be doing

a cross-country run this week, but my hip hurt too much so I had to stay at school and do work instead.'

'Oh, dear.' Abby made a face. 'Do you like cross-country running?'

'Yeah. It's better than doing maths.'

Abby smiled. 'We'd better see if we can do something about that hip, then,' she said.

She went to study the test results with Helen. 'If you've ruled out all the main causes of hip pain, then it's probably a transient synovitis,' she told Helen. 'Usually we would aspirate some of the fluid from the effusion and send it to the lab, but unless it's anything major, I would leave it. It's probably caused by a viral infection, and as he's well enough in himself, I don't think we need to worry too much about it. I expect it will settle down of its own accord in a couple of weeks, as long as he takes care to rest the joint.'

'I'll give him anti-inflammatories, then, and arrange for an outpatient appointment, shall I?' Helen gave her a querying look.

'Yes. Make sure the parents let us know about any flare-up of the condition and give them a letter for their GP.'

'I will.'

Matt arrived back in A and E just as she was going to find Sam. 'I thought you had gone home a long while ago,' she said, looking at him in surprise.

'I did,' he said, 'but I had to come back for some paperwork that Admin was putting together for me. Do you think you could spare me a few minutes? I want to run something by you, and alongside that the admin department said you have a file of statistics that might be useful to me.'

'I'm up to my ears at the moment,' she said. She tried to keep the weariness out of her voice. 'It's been non-stop in here since you left, and Sam has been waiting to talk to me for the last half-hour. You can walk with me, if you like, and I'll answer any questions as we go.'

'Thanks.' He looked as though he didn't have a problem with that but, then, why would he? He wasn't struggling to deal with a dozen situations at any one time, and he certainly seemed to have time on his hands now that his TV series had come to an end.

She went to move off in the direction of the treatment room, but he stalled her. 'Are you sure you wouldn't be better off taking a break for a few minutes? You look as though you could do with a cup of coffee. It might help to revitalise you. Besides, you seem tense, as though your shoulders and neck are all knotted up. I do a pretty good massage, you know.'

She gave him a wry look. 'I've heard that one before.'

He gave her a mischievous look. 'Maybe, but I'm a proper doctor, you know, the real thing. Haven't you ever seen the intro to my TV programme? I don't just wear a stethoscope to wow the audience.' His blue eyes danced with flickering lights and his mouth made a teasing smile.

'You're out of this world,' she said, giving him an amused grin in spite of herself. 'I'll forgo the massage, thanks, but actually coffee sounds pretty good. I dare say Sam will hold on for a few more minutes longer. He said it wasn't urgent.'

They went to the doctors' lounge, and Matt made her sit in a comfortable armchair while he went and made the coffee.

'Real filter coffee,' he said, coming back to her with a steaming mug, sounding impressed. 'Smells good…' He took a sip. 'Tastes good, too. It isn't like the stuff you get in most hospitals where I've worked.'

'That's because I bring it in,' she told him. 'If there's one thing I like, it's a good cup of coffee.'

She sipped the aromatic brew and then closed her eyes briefly, savouring the moment of relaxation.

'You look as though you could sleep right there,' Matt said.

She opened her eyes. 'You're right, I could. We are so busy, completely overworked and understaffed. It sometimes feels as though I'm on a roller-coaster, going round and round endlessly.'

'I can imagine.'

'Can you? I would have thought it's a long time since you had to cope with the day-to-day stresses of the emergency department. Going around and about with a TV crew doesn't seem half as demanding to me.'

'It isn't that long ago since I worked in A and E. As to the TV work, it isn't demanding, I grant you, but it can be heart-rending. Some of the people we see are in a bad way. I can identify with them, just as I can with you and the stresses you feel. You do your job in an efficient, professional way, but I know you aren't immune from the emotional dilemmas it throws up. You couldn't help but feel empathy towards the young woman who was attacked by her husband, for instance.'

'Melanie was vulnerable, and her child along with her.'

'Yes, but so are you. I just haven't quite managed so far to work out in what way.'

'I'm not. I'm very grounded and capable. You're imagining things.'

'No, I'm not.'

'You are, too.' She looked at him, waiting for him to come back at her, but he stayed silent, his mouth making a crooked shape, and she said on a faint chuckle, 'It's your turn.'

'I know. I also know that you're trying to put me off track.' His gaze meshed with hers. 'You're not going to tell me what caused you to identify with Melanie, are you?'

She sighed. 'It isn't a secret.' She drank the rest of her coffee and then put down her cup. 'It was a bad experience and one that I would much rather forget, to be honest. The truth is, I was attacked at work one day by a man who turned out to be a schizophrenic. He had some strange idea that I was his estranged wife, and he picked up an instrument from one of the treatment trolleys and stabbed me in the abdomen.'

His eyes widened. 'I'm so sorry. That must have been terrible for you.'

She winced. 'At least I was in the hospital and help was close at hand.'

'There is that, I suppose.' He came over to her and

knelt down beside her chair so that he was on a level with her, looking into her eyes. 'It must have been difficult for you to come back to work.' He laid a hand gently on her arm and warmth flowed through her almost as though he was healing her with his touch.

She nodded. His understanding of how she had felt back then startled her. 'It was scary at first, but I knew that I had to face up to my demons. It was either that or go under.'

'I have the feeling that you would never let anyone, demons or otherwise, get the better of you.' His gaze was intense, compassionate, and she realised that she needed to pull herself together.

'You're right, and I should really go and tackle some of them now,' she said. 'I have to get back to work.'

'May I go with you? I'm fascinated by the way you handle the problems that come your way. You're always so bright and on top of things.'

'I'm glad you think so.' She nodded in acknowledgement of his question, and he stood up, letting go of her arm, so that she felt a chill of loss, almost as though he had cut a connection. She got to her feet and led the way out of the room.

He went with her in search of Sam and his patient. Sam was treating a seven-year-old child who had suffered an electrical injury.

Abby introduced herself to the boy and his mother. 'What happened here?' she asked, giving the boy a coaxing smile, but he didn't answer. He was pale and subdued, watching as the nurse dressed burns to his hands and Abby guessed that he wouldn't be easily distracted while that was going on.

'Callum was playing with a fort that his dad made for him,' Sam told her. 'It had lights supplied by a cable that was plugged into the electrical socket, and he decided that the plug didn't need to be attached any more.'

'Ouch.' Abby winced. 'That obviously had painful consequences. How did he manage to remove it? And why would he want to do that?'

'It was in the way,' the boy said, looking up from having his hands dressed. 'It wouldn't tuck back into the roof space and I wanted the roof to be flat, so I got some scissors and cut it off.' He paused momentarily. 'It went bang.'

'It did?' Abby's eyes widened.

'It certainly did,' his mother put in. 'We all heard it. And then he must have fallen back and banged his head on the bunk bed. When we rushed into the bedroom to see what was going on, we found him unconscious on the floor. We didn't know whether he was knocked out from the fall or from the electric shock.'

Abby looked at the boy. 'So you didn't think to switch the electricity off at the plug before you took the scissors to the cable?'

The boy shook his head and made a grimace. 'I forgot.'

'Well, that would certainly do it,' Abby said. She turned to Matt. 'It has to be a boy who would do something like that, doesn't it?' she said in a soft tone. 'They always seem to be getting ideas into their heads about how to fix things…or unfix them, as the case may be.'

'It's because we like to find answers to problems,' he said, with a smile for her alone. His blue gaze flickered as it swept over her features. 'Give a boy a puzzle and he'll work on it until he's managed to figure it out.'

'Hmm.' She wasn't sure she was happy with the way he looked at her when he said that. Did he think she was a puzzle, an enigma that he needed to solve?

She turned to Sam. 'You wanted to ask me about something?' She kept her voice low, and studied the boy's chart while Sam drew her attention to the heart trace.

'There was an upset with his heart rhythm when he was brought in. I'm not sure whether it was because of the electrical shock or from some other cause. There appears to be a slight murmur, too. Should I be doing other tests?'

She nodded. 'It's probably nothing significant… most likely it's the aftermath of a recent illness…but I would follow it up, without being too invasive, and arrange an outpatient appointment in a few weeks' time, just to be on the safe side. Keep him on the monitor here for twenty-four hours to make sure that the heart rhythm is back to normal.'

'OK, I'll do that, thanks.'

She spoke to the boy and his mother for a while longer and then left the treatment room.

She glanced at Matt. 'I expect you've come across this kind of situation before, when you've been out and about with the TV crew. Children often poke things into electrical sockets and end up in A and E, don't they? Is this the kind of event you would have put on camera?'

Matt studied her. 'Are you asking me in case I was thinking of bringing a crew in here at some point?'

She laughed. 'That's about as likely to happen as you putting in an application for the part-time job here.'

He mused on that. 'Actually, that isn't as farfetched as it might sound. I'd be prepared to think quite seriously about coming to work here on a part-time basis now that my TV series has come to an end. We might even consider making a deal on that score...I'll work here in exchange for you agreeing to a few programmes being filmed. After all, you said yourself that you were overworked and understaffed. I'm up to date with emergency work, and I've specialised in paediatrics... And you still don't have anyone to fill the vacancy, do you?'

That was an underhanded move, wasn't it? He knew full well how desperate they were to find a competent doctor to fill the slot, and what were the odds that Helen had filled him in on their progress to date? The woman was way too eager to have him around.

'Even so, I don't know that a deal is on the cards,' she said. 'It goes against the grain to have cameras intruding on the unit, and I'm sure the hospital management wouldn't agree to it.'

'Actually, Admin are all for the idea. It would bring money to the hospital and help the public to see how important your work is here. I could throw in a few pointers about preventative medicine, too. You'd want to be able to help people, wouldn't you?'

She looked at him with narrowed eyes. 'So you've already gone through this with the bosses?' She might have known he would do that. She sucked in her breath. 'How many programmes did they agree to?'

'Twelve,' he said.

She gritted her teeth in annoyance, and then shook her head. 'That's way too many. I wouldn't be able to cope with the chaos.'

'Make it six,' he suggested. 'And I would work five mornings a week, so that I can keep the afternoons free for my feature writing and the scripts for the radio broadcasts? How does that sound?'

'It sounds,' she said crisply, 'as though you've been cooking this up with management behind my back for some time, and now you've cleverly backed me into a corner.' She glowered at him. 'Anyway, I thought your radio programme goes out in the morning?'

'It does, but we record them before breakfast-time, so they don't actually go out live.' He sent her an encouraging look. 'I don't see that as a problem. I would still be able to get here early enough for the morning shift.'

The thought that he was willing to work in A and E weighed heavily in the balance. They needed another doctor in the unit and she knew that he was more than competent, from what she had seen and heard. His qualifications were there for all to see on his website, and they were very impressive.

What real choice did she have? 'You had better leave your CV with Personnel. They'll sort everything out as to hours and salary.'

'That's brilliant.' His mouth curved and he leaned towards her and before she had any idea what he was about, he had planted a kiss firmly on her lips. 'I knew you'd come around to my way of thinking.'

She was too stunned to say a word. Her heart was

racing and her lips were still tingling from the tumul-
tuous effect of that brief kiss when he stopped and
glanced at his watch. 'I'm glad we sorted that out,' he
said, 'but I have to go now, or I shall be late.'

She stared at him. He wasn't at all fazed by that
moment of intimacy. As far as he was concerned, it
might never have happened, it had been a momentary
impulse. Whereas, for her part, she was finding it dis-
tinctly hard to recover her equilibrium. He had kissed
her. He had actually kissed her and her lips were on
fire.

Somehow she managed to find her voice. 'Late for
what?' she asked. 'Another recording?'

He shook his head and said distractedly, 'No. I said I
would pick up the children from their friends' house and
take them swimming, and I'm going to have to rush to
get there in time.' He glanced at her, already on the move.
'You won't regret this, you know. Things will be a lot
easier for you around here with an extra doctor on the
team.'

Her mind was buzzing with questions. Children?
What children? Was he married? She tried to form the
words to ask him, but he was already walking briskly
away from her, heading for the exit. Abby stared at his
disappearing back. Why did it bother her so much that
he might be a married man with a family of his own?

She felt every bit as though she had been involved
in a collision with some kind of earthmoving equipment. He had scooped her up and carried her along
with him and had somehow persuaded her to do something that went against everything she believed in. How
had he managed to do that?

He seemed to think that she wouldn't regret taking him on, but that was a false supposition for a start. She was already convinced that she had taken leave of her senses.

How could he send her pulses sky rocketing one minute and then bring her down to earth with such an almighty bump just a few seconds later? And more to the point, why had she broken her own rule and let him get under her skin?

Men were not to be trusted at all…not ever.

CHAPTER FIVE

'Do I look all right with my hair like this? I could put it up, I suppose…' Helen was flustered, checking her hair in the mirror in the doctors' lounge and then gazing down at her footwear with indecision. 'And what about my shoes? Should I wear my other ones? What do you think? I always keep a spare pair in my locker, just in case.'

'I think that you look perfect, as always,' Abby told her with a hint of impatience. 'I'm beginning to think everyone around here has gone mad. I even caught Sam checking out his tie this morning and comparing it with one in another colour. No one is behaving as they normally do, and the camera crew haven't even finished setting up their equipment yet.'

'I know, but they're working on it. They were holding a meeting first thing to decide which areas they were going to cover, and now they're going through the list of patients who have come in already this morning to see who they're going to include in the show.'

Abby swallowed the remains of her coffee and scowled over the rim of the cup. 'I shall be glad when they've done what they have to do and packed up their gear to leave. I still can't believe that I agreed to any of this.'

'But it's so exciting, Abby.' Helen's expression was animated, her eyes glowing. 'I was talking to the cameraman a little while ago, and he says the programme will be aired in just a few days' time. Just imagine…our own A and E unit featured on television.'

'And all the staff looking nervous, or overwhelmed and forgetting about the patients they're supposed to be treating. The only one who will have any notion of what he's about is the man who started the whole thing, and he'll have me to answer to if anything goes wrong.' Her mouth made a grim line. Hadn't Matt used her to further his own career, just as her ex had done? Now she would have to deal with the fallout from that.

'It won't, though, will it? Go wrong, I mean?' Helen was suddenly doubtful. She applied a smear of lipstick to her full lips and then made a final check in the mirror. 'Right, I'm ready. Back into the fray.'

Abby followed her a short time later, going out into the corridor and catching sight of a camera team that looked as though it was heading her way. She froze. The wretched people were everywhere. She would have to find a different route to take her where she wanted to be. She swivelled around to avoid them and walked straight into a solid object, one that was living and breathing and exuding warmth and energy.

'Hey, there, what's the rush?' The voice was calm and faintly amused.

She was temporarily knocked off balance, but two strong arms reached for her and steadied her, and she looked up distractedly, to find herself staring into Matt's laughing blue eyes.

'I know we said that we were going to be working closely together,' he murmured huskily, keeping hold of her, his hands coming to rest at the base of her spine, 'but I hadn't expected it to be quite such a riveting experience.' He ran his glance over her. 'Not that I'm complaining, of course. This has to be one of the bonuses of the job.'

Abby was struggling to cope with the rush of heat that swamped her entire body. Her breasts were crushed against the strong wall of his chest, and her thighs were in collision with a part of his anatomy that she didn't even want to think about. She tried to compose herself.

'Yes, well, um…I think I can manage now, thank you. I um…need to go and find my patient. He should be arriving any minute now.' Her heart was pounding, and she couldn't think straight with his arms wrapped around her that way.

He gently extracted himself from their unexpected embrace, but still held on to her, albeit at arm's length. 'The baby with the projectile vomiting? I heard that he was on his way to A and E.'

Did he ever miss anything? She nodded. 'That's the one.' She glanced up at him. 'If you'd care to let go of me, I was heading for the ambulance bay.'

'Of course.' He released her and stood to one side, and she could feel his gaze following her as she started off along the corridor. Unfortunately, she also caught sight of the camera crew bearing down on them, and she had the horrible notion that they had homed in on their minor entanglement. She promised herself she would go and vet the footage just as soon as she could grab a minute.

It was bad enough that she had been involved in such a situation in the first place, but if Matt was married and his wife happened to see their encounter broadcast on the television, what on earth would she think? And what was Matt thinking of, flirting with her like that? What kind of man was he? Didn't he have any scruples?

She reached the ambulance bay and the ambulance that was bringing in the baby drew up a moment or two later. Abby supervised the transfer of the infant into A and E.

'I didn't know what to do for the best,' the child's mother said, looking anxious. 'He's never taken his feeds properly, and he seems to be wasting away. He's so tiny and he looks so ill. What's wrong with him?'

'That's what we're going to find out,' Abby told her. The baby was about four weeks old, and he was clearly dehydrated, lethargic and undernourished. There were also signs of jaundice.

Abby gently examined the infant. 'His fontanelle is depressed,' she said in a low voice to the nurse who was assisting her, 'and that's a sure sign of dehydration. We need to correct the fluid imbalance as quickly as possible, because he's already very ill.'

'Do you want me to set up a fluid infusion?'

'Yes, I'm going to obtain intravenous access so that we can do some tests, and once we know what we're dealing with we can correct the electrolyte abnormalities.'

She moved around to the other side of the bed in order to help set up the fluid infusion, and almost ran into the camera rig. She looked up, startled to see that she was being filmed, but she quickly swallowed her irritation. Her main priority right now was to help this little boy back to health.

'You said that he's dehydrated,' the mother queried. 'Is that bad? Like I said, I've tried to feed him but he won't keep anything down.'

'It isn't your fault,' Abby reassured her, 'but when a child loses fluid, either through vomiting or diarrhoea, the kidneys have to work much harder, and they aren't as efficient as normal. The baby's whole system becomes unbalanced.'

'Is that why he has that yellowish colour?'

Abby tried to explain in a way that the infant's mother might understand. 'It's most likely because his liver is trying to cope with the extra workload.'

'Do you know what's causing all this to happen?'

'I think so,' Abby told her. 'There seems to be an obstruction in the outlet from his stomach that's preventing him from digesting his feeds properly. I felt it when I examined him, but I'll do an ultrasound to confirm it.'

'Is it dangerous?' The young mother was alarmed. 'Can you do something for him?'

'Yes, I'm sure we can. We don't really know why these things happen, but it's certainly treatable. It's probably caused by a thickening of the muscular outlet that allows food to pass from the stomach, which is easily cleared by an operation. It's usually a fairly straightforward procedure, and the surgeon will most likely do it through the umbilicus, so that there shouldn't be too much indication that he's had the surgery at all once it's healed up.'

'And will that cure him?'

'Yes, he should be able to feed normally a few hours after he's come back from Theatre.'

Abby did what she could to put the mother's mind at rest, and then she went to speak to the nurse. 'We'll call for the neonatal surgeon to come and take a look at the infant, but I think she'll want to make sure that the fluid balance is restored before she does anything at all.'

'So we'll admit him to the observation ward for the next few hours?'

'Yes. He can stay there until he goes for surgery.'

She left the treatment room and had to wait while the cameraman backed the rig out of the way. Her mouth made what she hoped looked something like a smile, but she was sorely tempted to grit her teeth. Matt had a lot to answer for.

She would have liked to give him a piece of her mind, but he was working with a patient when she went by the trauma room, and she contented herself with looking in on him to see how things were progressing.

He was busy resuscitating a child who had collapsed earlier that morning, and Abby had to admit that he certainly seemed to know what he was doing. The girl was on a heart monitor, and Matt left her side to go and ring for a cardiac surgeon.

He looked across the room and saw Abby as he replaced the receiver on its base. 'She has a valve problem,' he told her. 'Once we have that sorted out, she'll be back on her feet again.'

'I'm glad to hear it,' she said, keeping her voice cool and evenly modulated.

She started to move away into the main area of A and E and he went with her. 'Do I detect a hint of frost in the air?' he said. 'Or has management decided to save money on heating by turning the thermostats down? I thought you might be relieved to have an extra body on your team, but you don't seem too happy with the way things are going.'

'I might be relieved,' she agreed tautly, 'except that it came at a price.' She looked around to see if the cameras were still following her around, but thankfully they were nowhere to be seen. She glared at him. 'If I seem to be out of sorts it's because I've come to realise that you used me to get what you wanted. I'm definitely feeling touchy about that. I've had enough of men walking all over me to further their own ambitions, so maybe it would be for the best if we simply agree that we have to work together and aim to keep things between us on a purely professional footing.'

He nodded. 'Of course. I know that you had a raw deal in the past. Helen told me about the ex-boyfriend.' His blue gaze was sympathetic. 'That must have been a nasty experience, and it must have left a bad taste in your mouth. I'm not surprised that you're cautious around people but, believe me, I'm not about to make inroads on your territory. I just feel that you're doing such a good job here, and I think others should know about it.'

Was he patronising her? Her mouth clamped down

on a bitter retort. Instead, she managed coolly, 'Helen has far too much to say about things that don't concern her. She's an excellent doctor, but I'd rather she had kept that to herself, and I would very much prefer it if you don't go discussing my private life with any more of my colleagues.'

He gave her a startled look. 'It really wasn't like that, you know. Helen didn't spill the beans as such. I just made a comment about a research project I was interested in, and she made a throw-away remark that caught my attention. She was pointing out how hard you had worked on a project of your own, and I started asking questions. If anyone's to blame, it's me.'

'Yes. I already knew that.' Abby's green eyes flashed. 'You have a way of getting whatever you want, and that isn't all of it…any man who can flirt outrageously the way you do has to be blameworthy. It's one thing to charm the viewers into watching your programmes, but it's quite another to get fresh with female colleagues when you have a family waiting for you back home.'

He appeared to be stunned by what she said. 'I don't think I quite follow your train of thought. I wasn't getting fresh, as you put it. After all, you were the one who walked into me.'

She glared at him. How dared he turn the situation around and make out that she was the one in the wrong? 'Don't play games with me,' she said. 'I'm not in the mood.'

He put up his hands as though warding her off. 'OK, I can see that you mean business.' He looked at her more closely. 'Are you sure you aren't overdoing things around here? You seem very overwrought. Perhaps you should try to take a few more breaks between seeing patients, or aim to delegate your responsibilities a bit more?'

Her head went back at that. 'Are you trying to tell me how to do my job?' She heard the clatter of a trolley in the distance and absently moved to one side in readiness for it to pass.

'Not at all. You do it brilliantly. If anything, I think you work too hard and you need a complete break, a chance to get away from here and sample the delights of the open air. It's springtime, and I'll bet you haven't even noticed.'

Abby tried to hide a grimace. He had unwittingly hit on a sore point, hadn't he? When did she ever have time to stop and smell the roses, so to speak? By the time she left here she was usually too drained to want to do anything except go home. And then there were all the domestic chores that needed to be done.

He moved closer to her and draped an arm around her shoulders. 'I know a beautiful spot by the river near the studios where I record some of my TV shows. It would be the ideal place for a picnic. What do you say we try it out? I have to drive over there this afternoon to do a short interview piece, and we could find ourselves a sunlit grassy bank and make the most of the lovely weather.'

She wriggled her shoulder from out of his grasp. 'You're incorrigible,' she said in a taut voice. 'What makes you think I would even consider such a thing?'

'Well, because I think you could do with some time off. You were at work way before I was this morning, so I guess that you were either called in to see a patient or you came in on an early shift. Either way, I believe you're due to finish work by mid-afternoon, so you shouldn't have any problem getting away. What do you think? Shall we make a date?'

She looked at him, her eyes widening. 'What I think,' she said, 'is probably unrepeatable in polite company. How can you stand there and proposition me when you have a wife and children waiting for you to go home to them?'

He was silent for a moment, simply looking at her, with faint frown lines forming between his brows. She guessed he was trying to work out how to get out of the corner he had worked himself into, and she stared back at him, daring him to deny it.

Finally, he pressed the tip of his tongue thoughtfully across his lower lip and said in a wondering tone, 'Last time I looked, I didn't have a wife. In fact, I'm pretty sure that I'm very much a single man, footloose and fancy-free, unless someone slipped something into my drink one day and changed the situation when I wasn't looking. Bearing that possibility in mind, I suppose there's a slim chance I could be wrong.'

Now she was frowning. 'You said there were children. I heard you.' She waggled a finger at him. 'You said, "I have to pick up the children from their friends' house," or words to that effect.'

He seemed to be nonplussed by that, and a small frisson of doubt ran through her. He had been flippant in his answer, but that might have been just a cover. What if he had been married at one time but now he was a widower and she had gone blundering in with both feet? That would be unforgivable, wouldn't it?

He must have sensed her sudden tremor of doubt because he tilted his head on one side and looked at her, as though he was trying to work something out.

'That's very true,' he murmured. 'I did say that… and there are children, yes. Actually, I thought perhaps they might come with us this afternoon. School should be finished by the time you're free, and they'll be glad of the chance of an outing…especially a picnic. Jacob is seven, and he's into anything outdoorsy, and as for Sarah, well, she's just a year older, and she just loves watching the boats go by.'

'Oh, I didn't…I didn't realise that you might be looking after children on your own.' Why would he be doing that? Was he divorced, or separated perhaps…or, heaven forbid, was he a widower?

Abby tried to think back over what she had said to him. She had been slightly caustic towards him, derogatory even, and now she was beginning to wish she could backpedal. 'I…uh…perhaps I was a little hasty in what I said.'

'It doesn't matter. I can see how you might have misinterpreted the situation.' He gave her a coaxing smile. 'What do you think? Shall we have the picnic after all? I'll sort it all out. You won't have to do a thing.'

'Um…' Abby was at a loss to know what to do. Perhaps she owed him something after her outburst, and after all he was helping her out by working here, and he was turning out to be a godsend to the department. He was so skilled and experienced in emergency medicine that he was able to advise Sam as well as the junior doctors. It took a lot of the burden off her shoulders. 'All right,' she said. 'I think I'd like that. Thank you.'

A small cheer rose up from behind her and she turned to see that the camera crew had been following their every move. The colour flew to her face as she saw that the camera was actually focused on her. That hadn't been a trolley that she had heard trundling along the corridor earlier. It must have been the TV people.

Horror turned rapidly to annoyance and she glowered at the director. 'You will not broadcast a single scrap of that footage,' she told him. 'Or any of the filming you did earlier, out in the corridor.'

'That's a pity,' the director said. 'We've recorded some real gems up to now.'

A bright spark from amongst the crew chimed in, 'Instead of *A&E Uncovered*, maybe we should call it *Under the Covers in A&E*.' There was general laughter at that, and Abby shook her head in disbelief. Things were getting out of hand, and this was only the first day. What was the rest of the filming process going to be like?

She walked away from them and went in search of her next patient. The best thing she could do would be to lose herself in her work. She didn't even look back to see what Matt made of it all, but she heard him start to speak to the director.

He came and found her when her shift finished later that afternoon. 'I hope you're hungry,' he said, 'because I've packed up enough food to keep us going for a day or so. Just in case we get stranded out by the riverbank.'

She looked at him in alarm. 'I hope you're joking,' she said. 'Whereabouts is this riverside picnic spot?'

'I was joking.' He gave her a crooked grin. 'We don't have to go too far away. It's about a half-hour drive from here, but I need to stop off and pick up Jacob and Sarah first. Then I have to do an interview for a programme that will appear some time next month, but it shouldn't take very long for my part of the programme to be dealt with. They have a hospitality suite, and you and the children will be able to wait there if you want to do that. I believe you could also have a tour of the studios, if you'd like it. They're right next to the Thames, so the scenery is beautiful.'

'That sounds all right to me.' She hesitated a moment before asking, 'Do you think Jacob and Sarah will mind me going along with you? The last thing I want to do is intrude.'

'They'll love to have you with us. They're very outgoing children usually. Well, Jacob is at any rate. Sarah is a little more reserved, but she's a very sensible girl. I'm sure you'll get on really well together.' He smiled at her. 'You forget, I've seen the way you handle children here at the hospital. You're a natural. What surprises me is that you don't have a child of your own by now…but, then, you had problems with your ex, didn't you, so I imagine that must have made you wary.'

Her lips made a brief, taut movement. 'Let's not go there,' she said. 'I'd sooner forget that he ever existed.'

He winced. 'It was that bad?'

She gave him a concentrated stare, and he backed off. 'You won't hear another word from me,' he said. 'My lips are zipped.'

She chuckled at the image, and shook her head. 'Knowing you, I doubt they'll stay that way for long.' She was quiet for a moment, wondering about the children and what had happened in his life for him to be caring for them on his own, but after the mess she had made of things earlier, she thought it would be wiser for her to stay silent. He would tell her when he was ready.

'I'm sorry that you were upset by the camera crew this morning,' he said, as they headed out of the hospital towards the car park. 'I think they were just filming on the off chance of finding snippets of medical staff interaction, but it wasn't quite the kind they expected. I made sure that they won't be showing it— or at least that they will only broadcast stuff that makes us look like normal, caring professionals.'

He sent her a sideways glance. 'They'll probably show a tiny fraction of our first encounter, when we bumped into one another, but they'll edit out what was said and move on to where you told me about the baby who was ill. That will lead them into the part where you outlined his treatment.'

'Are you sure that's what they'll do?'

He nodded. 'Yes, the producer said he would show me the film after it was edited. They might also include where we met up after I'd treated the little girl with the heart valve problem, but only to show us talking like colleagues for a moment or two. They aren't going to include what we actually said.'

'Thank heavens for that. I would never hold my head up in public again.' She gave him an assessing look. 'Thank you for taking the trouble to sort that out.'

'You're welcome.'

By this time they had reached his car, and he held open the passenger door for her so that she could slide into her seat. The upholstery was luxurious, and there was a look of opulence about the vehicle, from the tinted windows to the smooth leather console and the gleaming instrument panel. Abby sat back and tried to relax.

He drove to the school to pick up the children, and Abby waited, getting out of the car to stand by it, wondering how the two young children would respond to her presence here.

'Hello,' she said as a boy ran up to her a moment later. 'Are you Jacob?'

He nodded. 'Are you a doctor?'

'Yes, I am. I work in Accident and Emergency.' She looked at him, noting the short black hair and the candid blue eyes that were the same blue as Matt's. He was a lean little boy, with thin, sharp features, and he never seemed to stay still even as she was speaking to him. He seemed to be full of life, as though he was ready for take off at any moment.

'Cool,' he said. 'Do you get to see the ambulances and the police cars? My dad says they put the sirens on when people get hurt and they go *wooowaaawooo-waaawoooaaa*.'

'That's right, they do. I see the ambulances when they bring people to the hospital and there might be a police car as well, but not very often.'

He seemed satisfied with that, and as Matt approached, Jacob tugged open the rear door of the car, bouncing with vigour into the child seat and scuffing the upholstery with his shoes in the process. Abby winced, but Matt didn't seem to mind, which was just as well.

Sarah was less exuberant, but she smiled shyly and said, 'Hello,' when Abby greeted her. She was a pretty girl, with long, chestnut-coloured hair, and Abby wondered if she took after her mother. Like her brother, her eyes were blue.

'We're going for a ride out to the TV studios,' Abby told her as she slid into her seat. 'Have you been there before?'

'No, but I've heard about them,' Sarah said. 'There's a river nearby, and a canal lock, where you have to open the lock gates to let the water through.'

'We might be able to do that,' Jacob put in. 'That'll be well good.'

'Yes, it probably will,' Abby said, with a smile.

They chatted to her as they made the journey to the studios, mostly about what they had been doing at school and what the teachers had said or done when someone had done something wrong.

'Jacob's teachers have a lot to say about this and that,' Matt said with a chuckle. 'He seems to keep them on their toes, one way and another.'

Matt was good with the children. He listened to what they had to say and asked about things that were important to them.

When they reached the place where the recording was to be made, he showed them to the gallery overlooking the studio where he was being interviewed. 'You can watch what's going on from here,' he said, 'or you could take a tour round the props rooms, if you like.' He glanced at Abby. 'I'll ask one of the secretaries if she'll show you around. She's always been very good about things like that, and she even offered to keep an eye on the children if I brought them with me.'

'Can we see the dressing rooms?' Sarah asked. 'There might be one where someone famous has been.'

'I imagine you could do that, providing nobody's using them at the time.'

Sarah giggled. 'I'd sooner go in when someone's there, because then I can ask for his autograph.'

'Well, there is that, I suppose,' Matt said cheerfully. He left them a short time later and they went on a grand tour, exploring the building as far as they were allowed, and looking out from one of the top-floor windows onto the landscape of the Thames and beyond. It was beautiful, with water eddying around small reefs of gravel and rock to form a weir, and in the distance there were swathes of green, where trees clustered together.

It seemed that it was no time at all before Matt rejoined them. 'Have you been OK?' he asked. 'Did you have a good time?'

'It was great,' Jacob told him. 'The lady let me try some costumes on and I dressed up as a wizard. And Sarah was a princess.'

'That sounds wonderful.' Matt's mouth curved with pleasure, and then he turned to glance at Abby. 'What about you? Did you enjoy looking around?'

'It was fabulous.' She smiled up at him. 'I've never been to one of these places before, and it was terrific fun to see all the sets, and realise that I've actually seen them before on programmes on television.'

'I'm glad. You certainly look more relaxed than I've seen you in a long time, and that has to be good.'

He was right. The experience had shown her how stressed she had been lately, and coming here with him had been all the medicine she needed. He had helped her to see that there was another world out there, one that she had forgotten about.

'Shall we go and find a place to have our picnic?' he asked. 'I'm starving.'

'That's a good idea.'

They went to Bushy Park and found a spot by Heron Pond where they could sit in the shade of trees and watch the wildfowl on the water. They were all hungry, and when Matt spread out a cloth on the grass and laid out the food, the children's eyes widened and Abby's mouth watered.

'I've brought fresh crusty bread rolls and there's an assortment of fillings to go with them—ham, chicken, cheese, and salad to have separately, if you want it. Help yourself.' He gave Abby a sideways glance. 'I made sure there are plenty of potato crisps and biscuits. Jacob and Sarah would live on them if they could. And there are cakes and fruit. Tuck in, or the ducks are going to have a feast.'

'Not until I've eaten mine, they're not,' Jacob said. 'They can have what's left over. I bags the cake with the blue icing.'

Sarah picked out a sandwich and gazed out over the water. 'I wonder if herons ever come here,' she said. 'I haven't seen one yet.'

'I'm sure they do.' Matt produced fruit juice and milk drinks and held them up for them to choose. 'Which one?'

'I love milk,' Abby said. 'Especially strawberry milkshakes. And it's delicious when it's made with ice cream, whipped until it's thick, and cold from the fridge.'

'I'll make one specially for you one day,' Matt promised. 'For now this is straightforward strawberry milk, but it is fairly cool from the ice pack.'

Abby sipped the chilled milk. 'It's lovely.'

He smiled. 'I'd have brought wine, but this is a family picnic, and I have to drive, and so do you, later, unless you're going to let me drive you home.'

'I'd better pass on that,' she said. She leaned back against the bark of the tree, content to watch the children eat the biscuits and start on the apples.

'Uncle Matt, can we play ball?' Jacob asked.

Abby's eyes opened wide. Uncle? Had Jacob said 'Uncle'?

Matt glanced at Abby and he must have seen her reaction to what the boy had said. 'If you like. I brought a ball with me. It's in the bag.'

Jacob went to rummage in the bag. 'Come on, Sarah. We'll play football.'

'Keep away from the water,' Matt warned them as they ran off to find a clear expanse of grass. 'And stay where I can see you.'

'We will.' Sarah waved as she ran to join her brother.

Matt took a sip from his fruit juice, appearing unconcerned.

'He called you *Uncle* Matt,' Abby said. She pinned him with her gaze.

'That's right. They're my sister's children.' He pretended to look surprised. 'Didn't I tell you that?'

'No, you didn't.' Her mouth made a crooked slant. 'You brought me here under false pretences, didn't you? You must have known I thought you had suffered some awful kind of loss, and it left me wrong-footed.'

'Ah, but I did tell you that I was single, didn't I?' He gave her a wry smile. 'I just happen to be looking after them while Amy and her husband are in Greece, looking to buy a holiday villa out there.' He sent her a quizzical look. 'Do you mind that I didn't tell you the whole story? Only I was afraid that you might not come with us, and I did so want to get you away from the hospital and have you all to myself.'

'No, I don't mind.' In fact, a little glow had started up inside her. He wasn't married, and he hadn't been married, and she was feeling good for the first time in a long while. 'I'm glad that I came here with you today.'

'So am I.' He leaned forward and kissed her gently on the mouth, brushing his lips tenderly over hers.

Abby was startled, but she realised that she liked the way he had moved in on her and she tilted her head a fraction so that she could appreciate the sensation for a little while longer. He gave a soft groan and deepened the kiss, winding his arms around her and drawing her close to him.

Abby loved the feel of his strong body next to hers, and her lips softened, tantalised by the coaxing, sweet exploration of his kiss. She moved against him, wanting this closeness, delighting in the warmth and reassurance of his firm embrace.

'Uncle Matt, we've lost the ball.' Jacob's piping voice brought her back down to earth with a crash.

Matt reluctantly let his arms fall to his sides, and Abby looked up and waited for her world to stop spinning. Jacob was looking at them curiously.

'It's gone in the long grass over there and we can't reach it because of the brambles,' Sarah said. 'Will you find it for us, please?' She pointed to where it had fallen.

'All right. Perhaps you'd better show me exactly where it is.' Matt gave Abby a smile as he stood up. He started off in the direction of the brambles.

Neither of the children went after him straight away.

'Were you two kissing?' Jacob wanted to know. He was studying Abby as though this was something he had never come across before and his interest was tweaked.

Abby didn't know quite how to respond to him and a ripple of guilt washed over her. 'Um, yes, I suppose we were.'

'Why?'

'Um…I think it just sort of happened.'

'Does it mean that you and Uncle Matt are going to get married?'

'I…uh…well, we, uh…haven't talked about that, Jacob. I really don't think so.'

Sarah dug her brother in the ribs. 'You're not supposed to ask that,' she said.

'Why not?'

'Because you're not.' Sarah grabbed her brother and turned him around, so that they were both facing away from Abby. Perhaps that way she thought they might not be heard.

'Mummy said Uncle Matt wasn't the sort to get married,' Sarah whispered. 'She said he likes to have lots of girlfriends and…' She stopped to think for a moment. 'And he isn't going to be ready to settle down for a long time.'

Abby pulled in a deep breath. The children had no idea that they were giving her such an insight into what was going on. Had Matt's sister worked out what Matt was all about? Even though he was half turned away from her, Abby could see Jacob's puzzlement. 'Settle down? Why?'

'Daddy says he's having too much fun as a bachelor.'

The boy's frown deepened. 'What's a bachelor?'

'I don't know.' Sarah was quiet for a second or two, mulling it over. 'It must be a special kind of doctor that goes on the telly.'

'Yeah, I bet it is.' Jacob sounded pleased that the mystery was solved.

Matt must have realised by then that the children hadn't followed him, because he came back towards them and said, 'I thought you were coming with me to show me where the ball had landed? When I turned around you weren't there.'

'Oh, we're coming now,' Sarah said.

Matt glanced down at Abby. 'Are you all right? You seem a little...stunned. I suppose that's the word for it. Has something happened?'

'No, nothing's happened, nothing at all.' She assumed a bright tone. 'I'm fine, really.' She got to her feet, adding, 'I'll come with you to find the ball.'

'OK, if you're sure you're all right.' Matt gave her a puzzled glance, but she put on a show of being her normal self and he eventually seemed to relax.

She gave herself a mental shake. It was true, wasn't it? She was fine. Nothing had really changed. She had been given a reality check, that was all, and it had pulled her back from the brink of disaster just in time. Matt was a single man, through and through, and any dalliance with her was purely that, a diversion, an uncomplicated way of passing the time.

CHAPTER SIX

'SO YOU went for a trip out to the riverside yesterday?'
Helen said. 'You had a good day for it, anyway. We
must have had the best weather for months.'

Abby's brow indented in a small frown. It was true
that her afternoon had been bathed in sunshine, but she
hadn't commented on her outing to anyone. 'How did
you know that I went out anywhere?'

She was adjusting the infusion pump so that the
child she was treating would get a slightly higher dose
of the drug, which would counteract the bacteria cir-
culating in her bloodstream.

Helen's mouth made a wry twist. 'I guess the grapevine has been working overtime. When you start going
out with a TV personality, you're taking a big risk if
you think you can get away with it without anybody
noticing. Don't you realise that people around here
watch Matt's every move?'

'I hope people would have better things to do, and
anyway I'm not going out with him, as such.'

Helen raised a sceptical brow. 'That's not what I
heard.' She reached for her patient's chart.

Abby made a face. 'So who's been talking?' She didn't want to reminisce about those few hours she and Matt had spent together, but the quiet time they had spent by the small lake had been uppermost in her mind ever since it had come to an end. It had been perfect, an idyllic time, except for the children's revelations about Matt's love life. She ought to have guessed that he would have a casual attitude to relationships, but perhaps she had tried to push that to the back of her mind. His kiss had put her head in a whirl and awakened feelings in her that she had not experienced in a long while.

After the picnic in the park they had gone for a walk by the lock, and she and Matt had helped the children to open and close the lock gates to allow the canal boats to pass through on their way upstream. All in all, it had been a heart-warming experience, and one that she would treasure.

'You and Matt were the ones who did the talking, apparently,' Helen said. 'Have you forgotten that you were on camera in the hospital yesterday?'

Abby was shocked. 'Any conversation was supposed to have been edited out.' Had that not happened? Helen was telling her that she was the talk of the A and E department, and that was difficult for her to accept. She had expected that her private life would stay that way, but clearly that was not the case. 'Are you saying that millions of people have listened to what we said?' The thought horrified her.

'No, you're safe, don't worry.' Helen chuckled. 'We just saw a rough cut of the show. Actually, it was Martin, the cameraman, who inadvertently gave the game away.'

'Did he? I can't think why the cameraman would want to let anyone know what I do in my free time.'

'I think he was a bit down in the dumps. Martin has the hots for you, haven't you noticed?'

Abby blinked at that. 'I can't say that I have. I've noticed, though, that some members of the crew would be more than happy to get to know *you* better... And I heard that one of the nurses has a date with the producer. This whole place has gone into meltdown.' She should never have allowed the cameras in here.

Helen grinned and added some notes to the little girl's chart. 'I had no idea that it was going to be such a pleasure to come into work this past week. I thought the first programme turned out really well.' She gave Abby a sideways glance. 'Some of us watched bits of the preview tape in the doctors' lounge, and we'll be able to see the rest of it later. Of course, seeing you and Matt on film, talking in the corridor on several occasions, was a bit of a give-away where the grapevine is concerned. I'm sure the outside world will think it was perfectly innocent, but we folks at the hospital know better.'

'They know how to gossip,' Abby retorted. 'All I know is that wherever I go, the cameras are lurking, and I shall be more than happy when they go and lurk somewhere else.'

She went to the ambulance bay to greet her next patient, and found that the camera crew had managed to catch up with her once again.

'Martin, could you not find something more interesting to film?' she asked, glancing at the man behind the camera. 'I'm sure Helen must be doing some really fascinating treatments.'

The camera made an undulating motion as though it was doing a happy jig. 'She knows my name… She knows my name,' Martin said gleefully.

Abby stared at him and shook her head in exasperation, her mouth making a reluctant smile. 'So, can we move on? I was asking about the prospects of you going to film Helen…'

'I would,' Martin said, 'but the director asked me to stay with you. He thinks you're perfect TV material.'

'He's making it up as he goes along,' Matt intervened, coming to stand beside her. His deep, gravelly voice coming out of the blue sent little thrills of pleasure coursing through her whole body.

She glanced at him. He was wearing beautifully cut dark trousers and his shirt was crisply laundered, a mid-blue colour that reminded her of a summer sky.

'Don't listen to him,' Matt said. 'He has a crush on you the size of a house.' He went up to the camera and mouthed exaggeratedly, 'Hands off. She's mine. I saw her first.'

Abby threw up her hands in despair. 'I give up,' she said, shaking her head and making the mass of her curls quiver in response. 'You've all lost your senses.' She went to meet the approaching ambulance. 'I have to work. Try not to get in the way.'

The infant that was being brought to hospital was a little girl, just six months old, and she was clearly having great difficulty with her breathing, even though she was receiving oxygen through a mask.

'Respirations are fast,' the paramedic said. 'There's a lot of wheezing and she has a slight fever. She's been like this for quite a while and she's getting very tired.

I'm afraid that she won't be able to sustain this level of stress for very much longer.'

'Thanks, Lewis. I'll do everything I can for her. Let's get her into treatment room two.'

As they were going into the room, though, the infant stopped breathing. 'I can't find a pulse,' the nurse said, and Abby immediately started chest compressions, using her fingertips to try to restore the baby's heartbeat.

Matt swiftly connected the electrodes that would attach the child to the heart and lung monitor, and the nurse took over the bag to mask ventilation that would maintain the baby's oxygen supply.

Abby glanced at the monitor. 'She's asystole.' Her heart plummeted. Defibrillation would be no use now that there was no cardiac rhythm, but she had to do something to bring this infant back.

'I can't get IV access,' Matt said a moment later. 'Her circulation has shut down.'

'Let me try. You take over here.' Abby handed over the CPR to Matt, and tried to gain intravenous access so that they could give medication that would help to resuscitate the child. After a couple of attempts, she had to agree that it couldn't be done. 'All right, we'll intubate her with an endotracheal tube.'

It occurred to her that Matt might have been put out by her taking over from him in such a peremptory fashion, but he didn't make any protest, and she didn't have time to debate the issue with him. The baby was her primary concern right now. 'Pause the compressions while I intubate her.'

Swiftly, she started the procedure, and then she

checked that the tube was properly in place in the baby's windpipe. 'There's good chest movement now,' she said. 'We'll put her on humidified oxygen to relieve the congestion in her lungs.'

'I don't feel a pulse when the chest compressions are stopped,' the nurse commented, a note of urgency in her voice.

'We'll go on with them.' Abby glanced up, and was glad to see that Matt had already started those once again. 'I'm going to give her epinephrine through the tracheal tube, and I'll take blood for testing through an intraosseous line. I suspect this is a viral infection, bronchiolitis, most likely, but we won't know for sure until the tests come back.'

'I still can't get a pulse.' The nurse was alarmed, and Abby could understand her apprehension. They had to do something quickly or they would lose this infant.

'I'm going to give her another dose of epinephrine.'

They waited for the medication to work, and the tension in the room was oppressive, until at last Matt said, 'We've a sinus bradycardia.'

Abby checked the monitor and felt a surge of relief. The heartbeat was slow, but it was a normal rhythm, and that had to be good.

'Blood pressure's coming up.' The nurse continued to give the baby the oxygen she needed.

'Heart rate's one twenty,' Matt said, some time later. He was smiling now, and the relief all round was tangible.

'That's great. Thanks, everyone,' Abby murmured. 'We'll give her bronchodilators to see if we can get the breathing passages to open up a bit more.'

They all stepped back after a while and went about their normal tasks. Some time later, when she felt it was safe to do so, Abby removed the endotracheal tube, and the baby made a little coughing sound and drifted into slumber.

Alone in the room, Abby checked the monitor and gazed down at the infant. 'You gave us quite a scare, sweetheart, but you're going to be all right now,' she said huskily. She lightly stroked the infant's downy hair, and smiled. She would have liked to cradle the baby in her arms, but the little girl had been through a lot and it would be best to leave her to sleep peacefully.

'You're deeply attached to the children in your care, aren't you?' Matt's soft voice reached her, and she looked up at him, nodding acknowledgement. She hadn't heard him come back into the room.

'Yes, I am. I know we should keep a professional distance, but who wouldn't feel the tug of emotion?'

'Is it hard for you to let them go?'

'When they're ready to go home, you mean?'

'Yes.'

She thought about that. 'I suppose it is sometimes. I'm glad that they're well, and ready to go with their parents, of course, but they always take a little bit of me with them.'

He nodded. 'It's hard not to get involved, but per-haps it's different for people who have children of their own. Then you might not tend to become so attached to them. Have you thought about that?'

'About having children?' He had asked her some-thing similar once before, she recalled, and she had fobbed him off then, but maybe having his niece and nephew to stay with him had made him wonder about family life. 'Yes, I've thought about it. Maybe it will happen some day.'

She said it on a soft sigh, because deep down she knew that day might never come. It wasn't just a question of finding the right man to share her life, but there was the nagging ache of that scar tissue left behind after she had been attacked. What were her chances of ever becoming pregnant? That was something else that she didn't want to have to think about.

He glanced at her, but perhaps he sensed that something was bothering her, because he left the subject alone. Instead he asked about the two-year-old girl who had been brought in to the hospital some weeks ago.

'I think her name was Lucy,' he said, 'and she was actually Sam's patient. You were very concerned about her because she had never been vaccinated and had an infection that left her in a very bad way. I wondered how she got on. Did she pull through all right?'

'Yes, she did, thankfully. It was a form of pneumonia, as we suspected. She was admitted to the children's ward and it was touch and go for a while until the antibiotics kicked in, but she finally went home last week. Sam was especially pleased that things turned out well for her.'

'That's good. I know Sam was worried, but it's always a great feeling when you see that they've come through the crisis point.' He looked at the sleeping baby and then sent Abby a swift glance. 'You made sure that this little one pulled through.'

'We worked as a team. That's what brings these

children back to health.' She gave him a troubled glance. 'I hope you weren't offended by my taking over from you with the IV access. I just felt that someone else needed to try before we gave up on it. I wasn't calling your skills into question.'

'I realise that. I would have done the same if I'd been in charge, but it's a fact that sometimes it's virtually impossible to get intravenous access.' He studied the monitor briefly before looking back at her. 'You know, Abby, you're a brilliant doctor and a wonderful paediatrician. You seem to keep a clear head, even when you're under pressure, and you guide your team well, whatever the task involved.'

He was thoughtful for a moment, as though he was trying to work something out. 'It can't have been easy for you to get where you are today. It must have taken a lot of hard work and dedication on your part, and it can't have helped when your boyfriend let you down so badly.'

Was that why he had backed off when he'd been asking about her wanting a family of her own? She had been thinking about the difficulties of ever achieving that, but he must have believed that she had simply been dwelling on the wrongdoings of her ex.

She gave a wry smile. 'They always say women have to work twice as hard as men to get where they want to be, don't they? I worked night and day to get the qualifications that would bring me to this position. I had to prove to myself as much as to others that I was worthy of this job.'

'Even so, it must have been a huge setback when your ex took your shared research and claimed it for himself. Was that before, or after, you came to work here?'

'It was before. I think it spurred me on to do something to convince myself that I wasn't a pushover.'

'What happened? How did he do it?' He hesitated. 'Do you mind me asking? I would have thought you would always try to keep your work safe.'

'I don't mind.' She gave a soft sigh. 'Yes, I did take care to protect my work, but I was recovering in hospital from being attacked when Craig went for his interview.'

She grimaced ruefully. 'He tried to say afterwards that he thought he was doing me a favour by claiming the credit for the major part of the work, as I was unwell and wouldn't be able to attend for an interview just then, but I was wary. I knew how ambitious he was. Me being incapacitated in the hospital was all the opportunity he needed. He wanted the promotion that I was going after and the kudos of being the lead researcher would help bring him that, so while I was recovering he put himself forward for it. He said we would both benefit from it, being a couple, because what was good for one would be good for the other, but I think he was trying to justify his actions to himself.'

Matt reached for her, curving his long fingers around her upper arms in an embrace that was comforting and sympathetic at the same time. 'That must have been a terrible time for you.'

She frowned. 'Yes, it was. I only found out the truth of what happened when his contract was cut and dried and I met up with someone from the interview panel who congratulated me on my small contribution to

Craig's wonderful research paper. I felt it was too late by then to do anything about it. I was hurt, and disappointed, but most of all I was bewildered. I would never have dreamed that anyone could do something so underhand, especially someone I cared for. And then I discovered that he had committed the ultimate deceit. He started seeing someone else while I was recovering from surgery, and that finished everything off for me. I was in hospital, trying to get myself together after a shattering event, and he was cheating on me.'

'I'm so sorry, Abby.' He ran his hand over her arm in a soothing gesture. 'It's no wonder that you're cautious around people.'

'I have to be.' She clamped her lips together momentarily and then said, 'I thought I knew him and it turned out that he was a snake in the grass. How can I ever rely on my instincts when I made a stupid mistake like that?'

His blue eyes darkened. 'He set out to win your confidence, and it wasn't your fault that he succeeded. People are not all like that. Someday you'll have to learn to trust again.'

Her mouth wavered. 'I suppose I will. Right now, though, that's a very hard thing to do.' Her expression was bleak.

He drew her towards him and bent his head, gently resting his forehead against hers. It made her feel safe and secure, having him hold her this way, and it was good to know that he cared. She felt the gentle warmth of his breath on her cheek, and more than anything she wanted to move closer to him and let her body mesh with his so that she could absorb some of his strength and unwind in the reassuring protection of his arms.

Only a moment of doubt crept into her mind as a fleeting memory of their time by the lake came back to haunt her. She was drawn to him more and more each day, but for her own sake she had to steer clear of any emotional involvement with him, hadn't she?

The children's innocent words should have been warning enough of that. He was having too good a time being a bachelor right now, and she would only be hurt if she let him into her heart. She had been burned once, and it would be foolhardy of her if she were to allow it to happen again.

She eased herself back from him. 'I envy Jacob and Sarah with their innocent take on life. Their world is full of joy and expectation, and they don't ever have to worry about being on their guard, do they?'

'Probably not.'

The baby stirred, and Abby glanced at her sweetly pink lips, and saw the way her tiny, dimpled fingers clasped the doll that she had brought in with her. She was over the worst. This was the kind of moment that made her job worthwhile.

She sent Matt a brief smile. 'They had a good time yesterday, didn't they? I expect they enjoy staying with you. Are they going to be with you for long?'

'Only for another day. Amy and her husband are due back home tomorrow.'

'You said they were looking to buy a property abroad, didn't you?'

'That's right. Last time I spoke to Amy she said they had found a villa that looked promising, but they were going to travel to one of the smaller islands off the coast to look at another couple of properties over there. They were planning on hiring a boat so that they could look around at their leisure.'

'It sounds wonderful. I've never thought about buying a place abroad.' She gave a brief smile. 'I have enough to cope with, keeping my small cottage up to scratch.'

His mouth tilted. 'Me, too. There's always something to do to keep the house looking good, and the garden would be a wilderness if I didn't tackle it every now and again.'

He sent her a coaxing smile. 'Actually, I wanted to ask you whether you would like to come over and spend some time with us at the house this evening. The children wanted to know if you would see them again before they go home. They really loved being with you, and Jacob especially is hoping that you'll play football with him and Sarah said she wanted to show you some of her drawings. She's a talented girl, but she's not very confident, and it would boost her if you were to give her some encouragement.' He lifted a dark brow in question. 'Will you come?'

'I think I'd like that,' she said. 'I enjoyed being with Jacob and Sarah.' She'd enjoyed being with him, too, but she wasn't going to tell him that. She couldn't quite find the courage to let him know how she felt about him.

'I'd heard that you live in a farmhouse,' she murmured. 'Is that right? Is there still a working farm connected with it?'

'There used to be a farm, but that went a long time ago. It's in quite a rural setting, though, because the house is in a valley surrounded by rolling hills and beech woods. I do have an original duck pond with a stream and a waterfall on my land, and it's great that the wildfowl still use it. The children love that part of the grounds when they come to stay, and at least now that they're older I don't have to worry too much about the danger side of things. I still keep part of it discreetly fenced off, though.'

Abby smiled. 'It sounds impressive when you talk about the grounds, rather than the garden. I'm envious already. My little cottage is what they call cosy. I've lived there for about ten years now, and I've sort of become used to it being cramped. I often think I should move, but I love little bits of it, and it's not too far for me to travel to work.'

'I know what you mean. That is always a major consideration.' He gave her a hopeful glance. 'So you'll come over to my place this evening? I'll make dinner for us. I thought we might have lasagne with sun-dried tomatoes, crusty bread and salad. What do you think?'

She gave a soft chuckle. 'I think you're trying to tempt me, and if that's the case, you've succeeded. It sounds wonderful.'

'Good. Then that's a date.'

A date? Abby felt a sudden quiver of uncertainty. Did she have any idea what she was getting into? Matt had begun to have a very strange effect on her. How else could she have gone from cautiously tiptoeing through life to reckless abandon in the space of just a few short weeks?

By the time her shift came to an end, she had given up on chastising herself. The deed was done, and she wasn't about to disappoint Jacob and Sarah if they had asked for her. The fact that she spent a long time choosing what to wear for the occasion didn't mean that she was trying to make herself look good for Matt, did it? She simply wanted to feel right.

In the end, bearing in mind that she might be called on to play football, she chose her favourite jeans, which fitted like a glove, and teamed them with a pretty top that clung where it touched and had a silky soft feel to it.

'You're just in time,' Matt said, opening the door to her a while later and giving her a wide smile. 'Jacob and Sarah have been busy making appetisers, so you're in for a treat. Fruit cocktail of melon, grapes, orange and apple, and an iced milkshake on the side, served up in dessert glasses. Specially for you.'

'For me?' she said.

He nodded, and whispered confidentially, 'I promise, I made sure they both washed their hands first.'

She smiled at that and then saw that the children had followed him along the hall and were looking at her expectantly.

'I can't wait,' she said. 'It sounds delicious.' They both looked relieved and pleased at the same time.

'I said we should make milkshake,' Sarah confided as they walked along the corridor, 'because I know it's your favourite.'

'It is. Thank you.' It cheered her to know that the children were happy to see her. Somehow it seemed important that she should get on well with Matt's family.

The children went on ahead, and Matt sent Abby an

appreciative glance as they went into the sitting room. 'You are breathtaking to look at—have I ever told you that? You make a pair of denims seem like paradise on earth.'

She laughed. 'Well, thank you for that.' He looked good, too, and she noticed that he had changed into casual clothes; chinos and a fresh linen shirt that was open at the throat to reveal lightly bronzed skin.

'I'll show you around,' he said. 'Shall we start with the upstairs and work our way down?'

'That sounds fine to me.'

She was glad that the children went with them. Looking in on the beautifully laid out master bedroom, his room, and imagining him there, waking in the morning and padding barefoot along to the *en suite* bathroom, was enough to bring her out in a flush of heat. Jacob and Sarah's presence thankfully took away some of the intimacy of the moment, and their happy chatter helped to ease her tension.

Why was she so constantly aware of him? It didn't make any sense at all.

'There are three other bedrooms, so the children can sleep over whenever they like,' Matt was saying, 'and there are a couple more bathrooms so that we're not overcrowded, even if Amy and her husband decide that they want to stay overnight.'

The bathrooms were exquisite, gleaming with subtly patterned tiles and luxurious with glass and mirrors and gold fittings.

Downstairs was every bit as perfect. 'This is my favourite room,' Sarah said, showing her into the study. The furniture was made of pale golden beech wood, with smooth surfaces and shelving with glass-fronted units that housed delicate Italian glassware, and there was a large window that let in plenty of light.

'I like to sit in here and draw,' Sarah told her, 'because it's warm and light, and the sun catches the glass and makes it sparkle. It's so peaceful and calm...unless Jacob decides to come in and spoil things.' She sent a testy stare in her brother's direction and he stuck his tongue out at her in retaliation.

'They're always fighting,' Matt said, his mouth curving. 'I used to be the same with Amy, but we were the best of friends really.'

'I'm not friends with Sarah,' Jacob said. 'Not when she won't let me play with my toy soldiers in here.' He turned his eager gaze on Abby. 'They climb up on the shelves and hide in the cupboards, and sometimes I stretch a string from the top cupboard to the floor, so they can paraglide down to their base.'

'That sounds like a real adventure,' Abby said, her mouth curving. She glanced across the room at Matt and caught his smile.

Sarah pulled open a drawer and took out some sketches that she had done. 'This is the villa that my mum and dad want,' she said. 'I looked at some pictures and made this for them. They said this is exactly what they're looking for.'

'That's absolutely lovely,' Abby said, with genuine admiration. 'I like that beautiful archway and the flower tubs on either side.'

They spent a few more minutes looking through the drawings until Jacob became restless, and then they moved on. Matt put his arm around her, his hand lightly resting on the curve of her hip, as he showed her the restful sitting room that was tastefully furnished with comfy sofas and a wide, open fireplace as the focus of attention. She tried not to think about what his gentle touch was doing to her. All she knew was that rippling sensations started up in the region of her spine and travelled to her abdomen, where they settled in an effervescent pool of excitement.

Over on the far side of the room, by the fireplace, there was a large recliner armchair with its own footrest, and she could imagine him sitting there of an evening, his long legs stretched out in front of him, one ankle crossed over the other.

It was a satisfying picture that brought a faint tilt to the corners of her mouth until an errant thought occurred to her. Was he always alone, or were there other women who came here and shared his leisure time with him?

'Shall we go and eat?' he suggested, and the children nodded vigorously.

'Yes, I'm starving,' Jacob said. 'Do we have to have lasagne first? Can't we start with the chocolate pudding? I like that best of all.'

Matt wasn't having any of it. 'All the more reason to save it for last.'

They had tea in the big farmhouse kitchen, a lovely room with golden oak units and a dining area that looked out through French doors onto a landscaped garden.

'I like eating in here because there's a much more friendly atmosphere than in the dining room,' Matt said. 'To be honest, I very rarely use the dining room, unless I'm meeting some of the TV executives for a working lunch. There tends to be quite a number of us on those occasions, so we need the extra space.' He made a wry smile. 'I think they like to get away from the studios sometimes, so a visit to the Chilterns makes a change.'

It was a happy, noisy meal, with everyone talking and sharing different experiences or reminiscences of good times. Abby was content, glad to be part of this loving family.

Afterwards, in spite of being full from the tasty food they had just eaten, they kicked a ball about in the meadow grass that formed part of Matt's farmland home. It was Jacob's idea. He had energy to burn, and Abby thought the least she could do was help him burn some off.

The phone rang when they were helping themselves to cold drinks from the fridge some half an hour later, and Matt went to answer it.

Abby could tell straight away that something was not quite right. Matt was careful not to say too much in front of the children, but even though he half turned away from them and spoke in a low voice, she knew that he was talking to a woman.

'I don't understand what you're saying, Kim,' he murmured. 'Slow down and say it again.'

Then he listened and frowned, and said on a cautious note, 'Are you sure? When was this? I don't see how—'

He broke off, intent on what the woman was saying, and then after a while he commented, 'I'll do that. I'll call you back in a little while.'

He replaced the receiver and stared down at the

phone as though trying to make up his mind about something.

Abby asked softly, 'Is anything wrong?'

'I'm not sure,' he said.

'Was it anything to do with the hospital? You're not on call, are you?'

'No, it's nothing like that.' He appeared to be distracted, and it certainly didn't appear as though he was about to tell her what was bothering him.

'Is there any way at all that I can help?'

'No... Thanks, all the same. I need to sort something out.'

Was that something another woman? How could he change from being relaxed and glad to be with her one moment to this total abstraction she was seeing now, all in the space of just a few minutes?

Her brow furrowed. He hadn't continued the conversation with this woman. He was going to call her back, and that might mean that he didn't want to talk in front of her. Why? Was she in the way?

Abby didn't know what to make of it. Was it possible that the woman who phoned him was a former girlfriend?

'Perhaps it would be better if I started for home now?' she murmured. 'It's getting quite late, and I don't want to be in your way if there's a problem. Are you sure there's nothing I can do to help?' If he wanted her to stay, he would tell her so, wouldn't he?

'I'm sure. This is my problem. It needn't concern you.'

Abby stiffened. 'I'm disappointed you should feel

that way,' she said coolly, affronted by his casual dismissal of her.

Something in her tone must have seeped through to him, because he looked at her properly for the first time since the phone call. He frowned, but still he made no attempt to explain his remoteness.

'I'm sorry to bring the evening to a close like this,' he said briskly, 'but something's cropped up and I need to deal with it.'

'Yes, I gathered that much.' Her presence there was stopping him from doing what he wanted. 'Obviously you have a lot on your mind right now, and no doubt you and your friend will be able to sort things out between you. She clearly has your undivided attention, so I'll leave you to it.'

Tight-lipped, she turned away from him and went to say goodbye to Jacob and Sarah and then started to head for the front door.

He sent her an odd look. 'Abby, I think you must have got the wrong idea—'

'Really?' There was a frosty edge to the word. 'I don't believe I do.' She hurried out to her car.

'Abby wait…' she heard him say, but by then she had revved up the car's engine and she had no intention of stopping to listen to him. He was frowning as he watched her drive away.

It was only when she arrived back at the cottage that she realised she had done it again. She had acted on impulse and let her irritation get the better of her. When would she ever learn to keep herself under control?

CHAPTER SEVEN

'How is the young girl who came in with the heart valve problem this morning?' Abby asked, as she and Sam were going through his case notes together. 'Her condition was similar to the patient Matt was treating the other day, wasn't it?'

'Yes, she had a mitral valve prolapse, but her condition wasn't as severe as Matt's patient, so she didn't need to go for surgery. I thought it would be best to treat her with anti-arrhythmic therapy.'

Abby checked his patient's chart. 'Yes, that's good. She seems to be responding to the medication very well. Did Matt advise you on that?'

Sam nodded. 'I asked his opinion because he'd asked me to assist with his heart patient the other day. I went with that patient to Theatre, because Matt thought it would be helpful to me to see her case through, and he was right. The surgeon was absolutely brilliant, and once the girl's recovered from the operation she stands a good chance of leading a normal life.'

'It's always thrilling to get a result like that, isn't it? I'm glad Matt was able to show you the latest techniques. Cardiac cases seem to be one of his specialist areas, as well as his knowledge of emergency medicine. He's a real asset to have around.'

'I know.' Sam's mouth curved. He gave her a mischievous grin. 'You and he make a great couple. Not just from a medical standpoint.'

She raised a brow. 'Are you suggesting there's another?'

Sam laughed. 'You can't be serious. Don't you know about the gossipmongers around here?'

'You shouldn't take any notice of them.'

'If you say so.' Sam was irrepressible. 'Did you see his medical notes programme on the television last night? It was terrific viewing.' He clearly had a lot of respect for the latest addition to their team.

Abby shook her head. 'No, I missed it.' She gave a wry smile. 'I had lots of important things to do, like catching up on the laundry and making sure my carpets didn't disappear under layers of dust.'

Truth to tell, she had made a point of not watching the programme. She had been sorely tempted to flick the switch on the television set, but then she recalled how distant he had been with her over the last couple of days, and she had steeled herself to resist the impulse. She was becoming more and more aware of him with every day that passed, and it was worrying how much she craved his winning smile or a crumb of affection. There had been scant supply of either of those of late, but perhaps she had brought that on herself with her hasty, ill thought-out words.

Ever since she had left his house the other day, he had been remote in his manner, and she couldn't help wondering if it was more than their disagreement that had set them apart. Maybe he had moved on from her in his mind. Perhaps her indifference to him in the beginning had captured his interest, and she had become a challenge, simply another notch to be added to his belt.

'You missed a treat,' Sam enthused. 'He invited the surgeon onto the show, and it was really interesting to hear what they had to say to each other. You'd think something like heart surgery for children would be a subject you'd want to leave alone, but they made it into compelling TV, not just for medical students or doctors but for people whose children are sick, too.'

'I don't know how he finds the time to fit everything in,' she murmured, 'but I suppose he must have recorded the programme a while back.'

'Yes, I think he did.'

Abby finished going through the case files with Sam and then went to catch up on the rest of her work. Matt was examining a patient in the trauma room, and she made up her mind to avoid him as far as possible over the next day or so. People were already linking them together as a couple, and she would be foolish to let that situation go on.

Her good intentions were knocked for six when one of the nurses came to find her an hour or so later. 'The four-year-old who came in a few minutes ago is in trouble, and we need a team to work on him.'

'The boy who fell from the window?'

'That's the one. We think he has a fracture to the back of his skull. Matt is taking care of him. The parents are frantic with worry.'

'I'm on my way.'

She hurried along to the trauma room, expecting to find alarm and chaos all round, but instead everything appeared calm. Matt was talking to the parents as he put a drainage tube in position so that he could monitor the boy's intracranial pressure. 'This will help us to remove any fluid that might cause pressure on his brain,' he said, 'and it will give us an indication of what action we need to take to keep his condition stable.'

The boy was unconscious and already had an endotracheal tube in place to assist his breathing, and Matt was giving him beta-blockers to prevent his blood pressure from rising to dangerous levels.

He glanced up as Abby entered the room. 'Good, I'm glad you're here. I could do with an extra pair of hands.'

'You have them. What do you want me to do?'

'Put in a nasogastric tube and perform suction while I check for other injuries. He's been vomiting and I'm worried about seizures. As soon as we get him stabilised I want to send him for a CT scan.'

'OK. I'm on it. I'll give him the anticonvulsant first.' She quickly set to work. 'Have you called for the neurosurgeon?' she asked, keeping her voice low.

'Yes, he's on his way. The sooner we can send the boy up to Theatre to have the damaged blood vessels repaired, the better his chances of recovery.' He, too, used a quiet tone in order to avoid upsetting the parents.

The neurosurgeon arrived a few minutes later and checked the child over. 'He's as stable as he can be for now,' he said. 'Let's get him over to CT scanning right away. I'll take him up to Theatre from there.'

The parents went with their child, and the surgeon answered their questions as they hurried along the corridor.

Abby watched them go, experiencing the familiar ache of anxiety in her abdomen. Would the boy come through this unscathed? The next few hours were critical.

'You did a good job,' she said, turning to Matt as she tossed her surgical gloves into the disposal bin and rinsed her hands at the sink. 'You kept the parents calm and you went on tending to your patient the whole time. You didn't miss anything.'

'It's the end result that matters,' he said. He was drying his hands on a paper towel. 'All we can do now is rely on the skill of the surgeon and pray for a good outcome.'

She nodded. 'When I see a child in such a desperate state it makes me wonder if I would ever want to put myself through that. How could anyone love a child and nurture him and then see him suffer in such a way?'

'The key is not to think about the negatives.' His gaze rested on her, his blue eyes warm and sympathetic, so that her spirits lifted a fraction for the first time in days. 'I tend to think you would make a wonderful mother. You have that caring instinct, and you're a natural when it comes to talking to children. That's why Jacob and Sarah took to you so well.'

'I'm glad we all got along.' Talk of motherhood had brought a slow tide of dismay that threatened to engulf her. Perhaps her contact with other people's children was the nearest she would ever get to anything maternal.

She glanced around the room, and it dawned on her

that she was alone with Matt for the first time in days. The knowledge that he had been so withdrawn in his attitude towards her lately made her wary.

'I suppose they must have gone back home by now,' she murmured. 'Did your sister and her husband find the villa they were looking for?'

A shadow crossed his features. 'I don't know. I haven't heard from them.'

She frowned. 'What do you mean? I thought they were due to come home two days ago?'

'They were, but something must have happened to them. No one's had sight or sound of either of them since they went over to one of the islands.'

'Are you saying that there's been an accident?' Abby was growing more concerned by the minute.

'It's possible. They were out on a boat when there was some kind of freak storm, and they didn't get to where they were going. I'm still waiting for news.'

A shiver of cold ran down her spine. 'Oh, Matt, that's dreadful. How long have you known?'

'Since the evening before they were due back. I had a phone call from an estate agent friend of theirs who lives in Greece. She wanted to let me know what was happening.'

'I'm so sorry.' Without thinking, she moved towards him, sliding her arms around him and hugging him close. 'That must have been so awful for you... and for the children.'

Was that what the phone call had been about when she had been at his house that evening? She had misjudged him and stormed off, letting her doubts override her judgement.

'Do they know what's going on?' She glanced up at him, her fingers closing around his arms, keeping the warmth of contact. It seemed the natural thing to do, to comfort him and let him know that he wasn't alone in this.

'I haven't told them everything, yet…only that their parents went to look at another villa, and they aren't able to come home right now. I didn't want to upset them if there was a chance that Amy and Tim turned up somewhere, safe and sound. I don't know how much longer I can keep it from them.'

She reached up and touched his face lightly with the palms of her hands, caressing him, wanting to show him how much she cared. He looked so bleak, as though the life had gone out of him. 'You did the right thing,' she said. 'It must be so hard for you to know what to do.'

He bent his head towards her and she tilted her face to him and kissed him tenderly on his lips, compelled by an impulse to assuage his grief in any way she could.

He returned the kiss, hesitantly at first, his lips gentle to begin with, and then with a ragged sigh he kissed her deeply, passionately, hauling her against him as though he would drive out his torment and lose himself in possessing her.

Abby's head was in a whirl. Her soft, feminine curves were overpowered by the strength of his long, hard body as he held her fast, gripped in a maelstrom of fervent need that overcame everything in its path. His hands moved over her, seeking out the soft swell of her breasts, running down over the curve of her hips and tugging her against the hard cradle of his abdomen. Sensation coursed through her, suffusing her with intense, earth-shattering desire. Her body was pure flame, burning out of control.

She wanted this, she needed to have him hold her this way, but at the back of her mind she wondered if he was really aware of what he was doing. He had kept his sorrow to himself all this time, not sharing any of it with her, but surely he must have known that she would want to do what she could to lessen his pain and be there for him? Why had he shut her out?

An ambulance siren sounded in the distance, and it must have brought him back to his senses because he dragged his lips away from hers and held her for a moment, his body taut, his breathing ragged.

He was very still. 'I shouldn't have done that,' he said. 'I don't know what I was thinking of.'

'It's all right.' Abby tried to reassure him, lightly laying her hand on his chest and registering the heavy thud of his heartbeat beneath her palm.

'No, it isn't. This is wrong, it's out of order.'

'I'm sorry.' She drew back from him, shocked by his vehemence, but, of course, he was right. He had never said that he cared for her in any special way, and he didn't need her to comfort him. She was letting her emotions run away with her. What had just happened between them was out of the ordinary, born out of a moment of madness, and it didn't mean that his feelings for her were in any way different from before. He was going through a bad time, and he wasn't thinking clearly.

He hadn't told her what was going on in his life, and

perhaps it was none of her business. He clearly didn't want to share such deeply personal worries with her.

Even so, she hated to see him suffering this way. She sent him a worried glance. 'If there's anything I can do, you only have to ask.' A thought occurred to her, and she added quickly, 'I imagine the children are still with you? Are you coping all right? If you would like me to give you a hand in any way, I'll do whatever I can.'

He shook his head and pulled in a deep breath. 'No, I'll be fine, thanks. I've managed to sort everything out so far, and it's just meant making a few alterations to my schedule. What I really want to do is to go over to Greece and see if I can do anything to help with the search. I feel so powerless being so far away, but I realise it's impossible for me to go right now. Jacob and Sarah have friends they could normally stay with, but for one reason or another they can't both be accommodated at such short notice. I'll just have to liaise with the authorities by phone as best I can.'

'They could stay with me,' Abby said. 'I'm a bit tight for space, but I could put a camp bed up in the study and at least there's a garden for them to play in.'

He gave her a brief smile. 'Thanks for the offer, but I would still have to make arrangements for them to be picked up from school and looked after until you finish work.'

'Not if you went tomorrow. I'm off for the next two days and as it's the weekend they would be off school.'

'Yes, but I have to be on duty here.'

'I'll find cover for you. Sam will probably do it, because he wants the extra hours, or I could call an agency. Anyway, you don't need to worry about that.

We've managed before under pressure, and we'll do it again.'

'If you're absolutely sure?' He gave her a cautious look.

'Yes, I am.' She heard the rumble of a trolley bed in the corridor outside and the bleep of a monitor nearby. It reminded her that there were patients coming in and she had to prepare herself to treat them. 'I should go,' she said.

'Yes, me, too.' He paused. 'Thanks for that, Abby. I appreciate it.' He touched her hand as she rested her fingers on the door panel, and she wished he hadn't done that because it stirred her senses and sent them into disarray when she had only just managed to force them into some kind of order. A lump came to her throat. Why did she care about this man so much? Didn't she have any sense of self-preservation at all?

'I'll see if I can book a flight for tomorrow morning.'

She nodded. 'I'll go and organise the cover for you.' She glanced at him. 'What will you tell Jacob and Sarah?'

'I don't know. Probably I'll say that I want to go and look at the property out there and see if I can meet up with their parents.' He grimaced. 'Part of that will be the truth, anyway.'

'Yes.' Straightening her shoulders, she went out into the main thoroughfare. Thank heaven the cameras were nowhere to be seen. That would have been the final scrape along the edge of her nerves.

Matt brought the children over to the cottage well before breakfast next morning. 'I hope this isn't too early for you,' he said, 'but if I leave here right away, I'll make the early morning flight. That will give me more time to do what I have to over there.'

'That's OK.' She greeted Jacob and Sarah and showed them into the kitchen where she had put out some colouring books on the breakfast bar and set out some jig-saw puzzles that she hoped might capture their interest. 'There's a pot of glue and some brushes,' she told them, 'in case you want to do some cutting and sticking later on. I've some old catalogues that you can cut up, if you like.'

Sarah nodded. 'I like to do that. I cut out furniture and rugs and things and pretend I'm making my house.'

'That's a good idea.' She smiled at both of them. 'I thought you might like something to eat first of all, so there's cereals and milk on the big table in the corner.'

Jacob went over to take a look. 'There's all different little packets,' he said. 'Can we have any one we like?'

'Yes, of course. Help yourself.'

He didn't need any second bidding, and Sarah gave him a scornful look. 'He's such a peasant,' she said. 'He always has to rush and get there first.'

Abby's mouth twitched. 'There are two packs of each sort, so you won't miss out.'

She spoke to them for a moment or two longer and then left them to it and went to talk to Matt. 'Have you thought out what you're going to do when you get there?'

'I'll start with a visit to the emergency services to see what stage they're at, and I'll go and talk to Kim, the estate agent, to find out what Amy's plans were when she and Tim set out that last day. I might be able to retrace their steps.' His jaw clenched and she could see that this was intensely painful for him. He didn't want to give up on finding his sister and her husband, but there still hadn't been any news of their where-abouts and hope was fading fast.

'Take care, whatever you do.' She laid a hand on his arm. 'Will you ring me and let me know what's happening?'

'Yes, I'll keep in touch.'

He went to the table where Jacob and Sarah were munching on chocolate-flavoured cereal hoops. 'Will you be all right here, then, for now? I should be back by late tomorrow night, all being well.'

They both nodded. 'Abby said there's a play area near here and she's going to take us there later on.' Jacob's eyes were gleaming with excitement at the prospect.

'Well, be good while I'm away.' He gave them both a hug, and then swivelled around to face Abby. 'I have to go,' he said, taking a quick look at his watch. He squeezed her hand, drawing her to him and resting his cheek against hers for a second or two.

Then he hurried out of the front door and slid into his car, starting the engine and hitting the accelerator almost simultaneously.

Abby watched him go, but he didn't look back. She felt empty inside. He hadn't even kissed her goodbye.

She went back into the kitchen and put on a cheerful face. 'Would you like some toast?' she asked the chil-dren, and they nodded.

'Yes, please,' Jacob said. 'Can I make a robot with these cereal boxes? I could stick some arms and legs on him, and give him big eyes and a laser gun. Actually, it would be better if I had a bigger box. Have you got any straws for his antennae? And I need some silver foil and sticky-backed tape and—'

'I'll see what I can find,' Abby said. Her head was spinning already and it was only seven o'clock in the morning. This promised to be a long weekend.

Sarah was a delightful child, a sweet-natured girl who quietly organised herself and kept her head while others flapped around. She took one of the jig-saw puzzles and asked if she could go and play with it in the sitting room.

'Yes, I'll show you where you can set it out,' Abby said, showing her into the neighbouring room. She guessed Sarah wanted some space to herself.

'This is a pretty room,' Sarah said. 'I love the colours on the curtains and the cushions. They remind me of the flowers that grow in my garden back home. We have sweet peas that grow along the fence in summer, and they have all these soft pastels.'

She gazed around her, picking out the comfy settees and the writing bureau that stood to one side, next to the tall window. 'And there's a bookshelf, like the one we have in our house.'

'Yes, I love to have lots of books around the place.'

Sarah turned back to Abby. 'Where will we sleep tonight?'

'Upstairs. Do you want to see?'

Sarah nodded, and Abby went to fetch Jacob so that he could join them. 'I wasn't sure who would want to sleep where, so I thought you might like to choose,' she said. She opened a door and showed them into the first dormer bedroom. 'This is my guest bedroom, and it faces out over the garden. It's nice and quiet in here, and there's a little writing table with paper and pencils and a lovely flower patterned dressing screen, so I wondered if you might like this one, Sarah?'

The little girl nodded, looking pleased.

'And this is the room I use for a study,' Abby said when they moved on. 'It's a dormer room like the last one, so it's an odd shape where the window juts out of the roof space, but there's a lovely computer table in here, and cupboards and little drawers.' She looked at Jacob. 'I thought you might like to play with your toy soldiers in here. You brought them with you, didn't you?'

'Yes, I did.' He looked around and saw the camp bed with a canopy over it, the filmy drapes providing a subtle hide-away. His eyes lit up. 'It's a tent,' he exclaimed. 'This is mine. It has to be mine. Can I have this one, please...please?'

Abby glanced at Sarah, who nodded. 'Ok, then. That's settled.'

'Can I stay in here and play?'

Abby gave a small frown. 'What about the robot you were going to make?'

'Nah. I'll make him later.'

'He does that,' Sarah said. 'My mum says he wears her to a frazzle.'

Abby smiled at that, but her heart gave a little lurch as she thought about why Matt was going away, and she looked back at the canopy, not wanting to give away the fears that clutched at her. 'I suppose that's all right,' she said to Jacob. 'Bring your toys up here.'

Jacob rushed down the stairs to search for his soldiers, and Sarah wandered back into her room to take another look around. She fingered the delicate glass-ware on the dressing-table and picked up a hairbrush that Abby had placed there especially for her.

She said quietly, 'Do you think Uncle Matt will be able to find my mum and dad?' She looked up into Abby's face, her eyes clear and bright, and Abby was so stunned by the question that she didn't know what to do or say.

After a moment, she managed haltingly, 'I'm not sure I understand, Sarah. Your uncle Matt has gone to look at some properties out there, and he said he would see if he could meet up with your parents, didn't he?'

'Yes, but he said that so that we wouldn't worry.'

'What makes you think that?'

Sarah gave an awkward little shrug. 'Because he's kind, and he wouldn't want us to know if anything bad had happened to them.'

Abby sucked in a quick breath. 'Do you think some-thing bad has happened?'

Sarah nodded. 'I saw something in the newspaper. Uncle Matt had thrown it away, and he never does that until he's read it, but I found it in the waste-paper bin and I saw a picture. I couldn't read all the writing, but it was about the place where my mum and dad were going to, and there was a boat accident and it said the people were lost.'

Abby put an arm around Sarah's thin shoulders and drew her down beside her on the bed. 'Did you tell your uncle that you had seen it?'

'No. I didn't want to worry him. I know he was trying to keep something from us, and I know Mum and Dad were supposed to be home by now. Besides,

Jacob might have heard us and he's too young to know about it.'

Abby folded her arms around her and held her close. Sarah was just a year older than her brother, and she was talking as though she had the wisdom of years in her head. 'I'm so sorry that you've had to keep this to yourself,' she said. 'You're a very brave girl, Sarah. I know how hard it must have been for you.'

Sarah looked up at her, and Abby could see that her eyes were sparkling with unshed tears. 'Do you think he'll find them?'

'I know that he wouldn't have gone out there if he didn't think there was a chance. He'll look in places where other people wouldn't think to go. We have to hold on to hope, Sarah.'

'OK.' Sarah gave a little gulp and buried her head in Abby's chest, and for a minute or so her shoulders trembled faintly. Then she looked up and rubbed her eyes and said, 'You won't tell Jacob, will you? He'll be upset.'

'I won't.' Abby's throat constricted and she felt the sting of tears behind her eyelids. Some children had so much courage that they put adults to shame. Matt had so much to be proud of in his young niece.

CHAPTER EIGHT

'WHEN'S Uncle Matt coming home?' Jacob asked as he put the finishing touches to his robot next day. It was a lopsided creation, with foil cupcake-case eyes that were set slightly askew and legs made from cardboard tubes that ended in yoghurt carton feet. The arms were fashioned from pieces of plastic that had a pair of Abby's salad tongs taped to one side so that he could grip things when Jacob squeezed them. 'I want to show him my Super-Robo laser.'

The laser was a masterpiece of ingenuity, Abby had to admit, with a slim-line torch concealed in a cardboard wrapper that had a red crystal bead from Abby's jewellery box glued on to it. The bead glowed when the torch was switched on.

'Super-Robo's coming to get you.' He switched on the beam of light, aiming the crystal at his sister and menacing her with the tongs.

'Go away,' Sarah said. 'I'm trying to make a card for Uncle Matt. He's coming home tonight.' She glanced at Abby for confirmation of that.

'Yes, he is. I think it will be very late when he gets

in, though, so you'll be in bed. You'll perhaps have to say hello to him in the morning.'

'Unless he wakes us up to say hello,' Jacob put in. 'Or perhaps we could have the day off school so that we could stay with him tomorrow?' he added on a hopeful note.

''Fraid not, Jacob. Uncle Matt and I have to go to work tomorrow. I'll tell him that you'd like him to come and say hello when you're in bed, if you like.'

'Yes,' Sarah said. 'Ask him to do that…please.' She gave Abby a cautious look that spoke volumes, and Abby knew that she wanted to be the first to hear if there was any news about her parents.

'I will.'

Abby went on folding clothes into her laundry basket. She didn't have any news to tell either of them, because Matt hadn't been in touch. All day yesterday she had waited for a phone call, and the same again today, but there had been nothing. Maybe he was too busy to even send a text message, or perhaps the truth was that she was simply an afterthought and he didn't see the need to talk to her at all. She was the one who had asked him to call after all. He hadn't volunteered.

It hurt that she felt like an outsider. She wanted so much to be a part of his life, but as the days had gone by she had begun to realise that it was a false hope.

She settled the children in bed later that evening, kissing Sarah on the cheek and stroking Jacob's hair as he snuggled against the pillow. He smiled as she laid a kiss on his forehead and he was asleep within minutes.

The hours passed by and still there was no phone

call. Was Matt on his way back to them? Perhaps it had been too much that she should ask him to keep in touch. The mere thought that some harm might have befallen his sister must be weighing heavily on his mind.

She didn't go to bed, even though it was late. Instead, she had a soothing bath and changed into her nightwear, then she wrapped a soft robe around herself. She sat in a chair by the fireside and watched the flickering images on the television set without really seeing what she was watching. Occasionally she fell into a light slumber, but she always woke after a few minutes, too keyed up to sleep for long, waiting for him to arrive.

It was well into the early hours of the morning when she finally heard his car draw up outside, and she hurried to open the door to him.

'I'm so glad that you're back, safe and sound,' she said, ushering him inside the cottage. She gave him a hug, and he wrapped his arms around her in return and held her tightly for a moment or two. He didn't say anything, or attempt to kiss her, and when he released her she felt a sudden sense of isolation.

His manner was odd, as though in his mind he was detached from her, and to cover her brief tremor of unease she said, 'Shall we go through to the kitchen? It's warm in there and I expect you'd like a drink or something to eat.' She led the way, adding as an afterthought, 'I was expecting you back here hours ago.'

He gave a faint grimace. 'The flight was delayed.' He looked tired, washed out and frustrated and she guessed that his search had been fruitless.

She pulled out a chair for him by the table, but he didn't sit down. Frowning, she studied him surreptitiously and wondered if he was keeping something back. Perhaps he couldn't bring himself to say what was on his mind.

'Is there no news?' she asked.

He shook his head. 'I hired a car and went over every inch of the area that they had covered. I checked the village the boat had been heading for and several places along the coast in either direction. There was nothing, no sign of them.'

She pressed her lips together, making a grim shape. 'I'm sorry.' She shook her head. 'I keep saying that, but I don't know how else to put it. It's a wretched business. You must be at the end of your tether.' What could she say that would be of any use? Not knowing what had happened, one way or the other, was a numbing state of affairs.

She saw the shadows beneath his eyes and wanted to comfort him. 'Would you like a hot drink? I could make you some hot chocolate—that might help you to get a good night's sleep, and then things might not seem so bad in the morning. What about something to eat?'

'I'm not hungry, thanks all the same. But I will have a hot drink, and then I'll slide into an armchair and get some rest, if you don't mind. I'm whacked out and I have to be at work in the morning.'

'You won't need to sleep in a chair. I've made up a camp bed for you in the sitting room. It shouldn't be too uncomfortable, because there's a reasonably good mattress on it.' She frowned. 'As for work, you don't have to go in. You won't be fit for anything after just a few hours' sleep. Don't worry about it, I'll sort something out.'

He nodded briefly, acknowledging the offer. 'We'll see in the morning. I'll go and look in on Jacob and Sarah, if I may. Have they been all right?'

'Yes, of course you may, and they've been wonderful. They wanted you to wake them when you came in.' She hesitated, running her tongue over dry lips. 'You didn't know it, but Sarah had guessed that something was wrong. She saw the article in the newspaper you threw away.'

He winced, and then pulled in a deep, shuddery breath, straightening his shoulders as though he was steeling himself for what was to come.

'Thanks for warning me. I'll go and have a word.'

She went into the kitchen and made some hot chocolate while he went to see the children. When he came back downstairs some time later, she pushed a steaming mug in front of him, and he sat down in a chair by the table and sipped gratefully.

'How did it go?' she asked him. 'With the children, I mean.'

'Not so bad. I told Sarah that no news is good news, and she seemed to be satisfied with that for the time being. Jacob was a sleepyhead. He gave me a smile and mumbled something about Robo-laser and then drifted back to sleep.'

She made a rueful smile. 'You have that joy to come. He's been working on it all weekend, so you had better make sure that you make all the right noises when you see it.'

'I'll do that.' Weariness washed over him, and she guessed that he had been on the move for the whole of the time he had been away.

'You should get some rest,' she said. 'I'll go upstairs now, and I'll see you in the morning.'

He nodded. 'Thanks for everything, Abby.' He went with her to the door and as she would have gone out into the hallway, he put out his arms to her and drew her close. 'It's good to come back and find you here. I feel as though you're the one person I can depend on. It means a lot to me, having your support.' He lowered his head to her and kissed her tenderly, making her whole body quiver in startled response.

It was over as soon as it had begun, and she realised that she had to take it for what it was…a gesture of thanks, nothing more.

In the morning, she was up and about early, getting the children ready for school.

'You've been a real help to me this morning, Sarah,' she said, as she finished clearing away the breakfast crockery.

Sarah's smile was tinged with sadness as she carefully stacked plates in the dishwasher. 'I do this for my mum every morning so that we can be ready on time. No matter how organised we are, we still end up rushing around at the last minute because Jacob always forgets something, or he discovers that he's lost his schoolbag or whatever. Last time he started hunting for something to talk about at show-and-tell time at school.'

'That's boys for you…' Abby said with a smile. 'Which reminds me…where is he? I sent him to fetch his bits and pieces ten minutes ago.'

'He's showing Uncle Matt his robot. I told him he wasn't supposed to wake him because he was very tired, but he said he was going to creep into the room just to see if he was awake. And then I heard them talking.'

Jacob came bounding into the kitchen. 'Uncle Matt was already up,' he said. 'He thinks my robot is the best ever. He said so.'

Matt followed the boy into the room. 'We have just five minutes to get all your things into the car,' he said. 'Jump to it.'

Abby looked at him and blinked. He was immaculately dressed in a dark grey suit, and his jacket was open to reveal a fresh white shirt underneath. 'I thought you were going to have a lie-in?'

He shook his head. 'No, I'm ready to go. Is there any toast left, or has it all been scoffed?'

She pointed to a plate on the worktop. 'That's going spare.'

'Good. I'll eat it on the move.' He grabbed a slice and bit into it. 'I'll drop the children off at school and see you at work in a while.'

'OK.'

A couple of minutes later Matt and the children piled out of the house and silence descended. Abby stared about her at the empty kitchen. It felt as though all the warmth had gone out of her life.

She arrived at the hospital a short time later, in time to see Helen going through the list of patients with the triage nurse.

'Ah, there you are,' Helen said, looking up and throwing her a quick smile. 'We've a boy coming in, five years old, with a rash and abdominal and joint pains. He's been vomiting. The family doctor called for an ambulance to bring him in.'

'Let's clear treatment room one for him, then. I'll take him and call for assistance as necessary.'

Helen nodded. 'I think the cameras will be following you around with that one. Martin and the producer have already had their heads together over which cases to cover.'

Abby winced. 'Tell me they're not going to be here for much longer.'

Helen grinned. 'I would, but I'd probably be lying.' She handed the list back to the nurse and came over to where Abby was going through a pile of test results at the desk. 'How did things go over the weekend? You said you were going to be looking after Matt's niece and nephew, didn't you? Did you cope all right?'

'Yes, it all went very well, considering that I'm not really used to having children around me at home. They're lovely, and very individual in their outlooks. I think they had a good time. I know I liked having them with me.'

Helen gave her a glance from under her lashes. 'You sound a little wistful. Has it made you feel broody, having them stay with you?'

Abby thought back to the evenings when she had tucked them into bed. There had been something about seeing the children snuggle down under the covers that had touched her heart, and a special moment when she'd looked in on them and saw them fast asleep, their lashes dusting their soft cheeks.

'I think it has,' Abby admitted. 'They can be so full of fun, or quiet and thoughtful, and I feel I'm missing out on so much. I just don't know whether it's something I'll ever be able to experience on a personal level.'

Helen frowned. 'Because of what happened to you when you were attacked?'

Abby nodded. 'It's always been there at the back of my mind ever since they told me at the hospital that I might have problems conceiving. The scar tissue could have messed things up.'

'Did you never get yourself checked out properly?'

'No. I think I've been afraid to, in case they confirm my suspicions once and for all. Anyway, it isn't going to be relevant in the immediate future.'

'Even so, it must be like a cloud hanging over you the whole time. Perhaps if you went for a scan they would be able to tell you if things have changed and the scar tissue has broken down, or whether there are new surgical techniques that might help to put things right. If it was me, I don't think I would be able to live with the uncertainty for long.'

'You're probably right.' Abby was still doubtful. Could she handle a definite negative answer?

'I could make the appointment for you, if you like. I know the woman who does the scans, and I'm sure she'll find time to fit you in as you're already on the premises.'

'Well, I suppose so…but I'm not sure if I really want to know one way or the other.' How would she feel if it was bad news? Would there be any future for her in any relationship if she couldn't have children?

Did Matt want children? An image of a little boy with black hair and an open smile that was essentially Matt's came into her mind, followed by that of a sweet-faced girl with dark hair and blue eyes. A rush of heat ran through her. How far she had come in these last few weeks, to go from not wanting to get involved with any man to thinking in terms of being with Matt for the rest of her life?

Was she losing all sense of reality? He didn't go in for long-term relationships, did he? And he wasn't giving her any indication that he wanted anything more from her than a brief dalliance.

'I'll make the appointment anyway,' Helen said, cutting into her thoughts, 'otherwise you'll go on dithering about it for evermore. Trust me, it's the right thing to do.'

Abby might have argued further, except that the nurse came to tell her that her patient had arrived, and she hurried away to the treatment room to assess the little boy.

Matt was just coming into the unit from the triage desk, and she caught a glimpse of his preoccupied, taut expression before he realised that she was walking towards him.

His features lightened. 'Do you need some help?' he said, coming to join her. 'Sam's busy with another patient, but I'm free just now. I'm waiting for a trauma patient who's on his way in.'

She nodded to him. 'Thanks. You could take the lead, perhaps, while I talk to the parents. Are you sure you're all right to work?'

'I'm fine.'

They went into the treatment room and Abby could see right away that the boy was in a sorry state. He was tearful and irritated by the rash, which had spread over his legs, arms, lower back and face. It was also on his buttocks, she discovered.

She nodded to the parents who were waiting by the

bedside, looking distressed and apprehensive. As the rash was a purplish colour, she could understand their concern.

The camera crew appeared and homed in on Matt as he went to talk to the boy. He looked up at the camera rig and seemed surprised to see that the lens was focused on him.

Abby gave him a mischievous smile, and as he glanced at her she mouthed, 'Your turn.' Under her breath, she said, 'Now you know how it feels to be on show when you're actually trying to work with patients.'

He gave a rueful grin and went to examine the five-year-old.

The child took no notice of the crew at all and she guessed he was too ill to care.

'Hello, Jack,' Matt said, going to the boy's bedside and giving him a cheerful smile. 'I'm Matt, and this is Abby. We're both doctors, and we've come to have a look at you so that we can help you to feel better. Can you tell me where you're hurting?'

'It hurts when I walk,' Jack said. 'My knees are all swelled up.'

'May I have a look?' Jack nodded, and Matt examined him carefully. 'Yes, I can see they are,' he murmured, gently testing the movement of his limbs. 'Your ankles are puffy as well, aren't they?'

Jack nodded miserably. 'And my tummy hurts.'

Matt nodded, showing the child that he understood. He was gentle with the boy, Abby thought, and seemed to have empathy with him so that the child was happy to have Matt looking after him.

She cast a glance over the admission notes. 'He's had a recent streptococcal infection,' she murmured, 'but there's no history of any other problems. The GP gave him an injection of antibiotics before he sent him here.'

'Good.' Matt turned back to the boy. 'We'll have to do something to stop all this, won't we?' He gave him a sympathetic glance and lightly patted his hand before going to talk to the nurse.

'We'll do a full blood count, urea and electrolytes,' he said, 'and we need to do an analysis of his urine. I'll write out the forms.'

Abby went to talk to the parents.

'Does he have meningitis?' The child's mother was trying to keep her anxiety hidden from the boy, but she was very stressed. 'That was why the doctor gave him an injection of antibiotics, wasn't it?'

'That's right. He did it to make sure that we've taken action from the earliest possible moment. We'll continue with the antibiotics here, as a precaution, but I'm not convinced that it's meningitis we're dealing with. From the look of things he's suffering from an allergic reaction caused by the throat infection he had recently. He's feeling very poorly at the moment, because it's brought about an inflammatory reaction, leaving him with a type of arthritis in his joints.'

The boy's father sucked in his breath. 'Arthritis? Will it be permanent? He's too young for that, isn't he?'

'Hopefully, we'll be able to treat the original infection that caused the problem, and as long as he gets plenty of bed rest he should start to recover and lead a normal life. At the moment we're more concerned about the effect all this is having on his kidneys, so once we have the test results back we'll probably start him on steroids and immunosuppressive therapy. We do see a few children of his age who come in with this type of reaction.'

The cameraman swivelled the lens towards the little boy and after a minute or two drew back again. Matt did a piece to camera about the type of illness and how long it would be before the child was up and about again.

'The disease is usually self-limiting, so we would hope that he might be back to his usual self after a few weeks. It really depends on whether or not there are any complications.'

Matt went on to explain how the treatment would help to get Jack back on his feet, and he talked about how to tell the difference between different types of rashes. Abby could see how his words would offer comfort to any other parents who were going through the same anxieties and give them practical information to show them how to deal with a sick child. She frowned. Perhaps she had been wrong in making such a blanket condemnation of these programmes.

Matt left the room with her a little later when he had reassured Jack and his parents that the situation should improve before too long.

'Poor little scrap. He looked wretched, didn't he?' He sent her a sideways glance.

'He did, but I think you managed to cheer him up a bit.' Her mouth made a crooked twist. 'I never thought the day would come, but I have to say that you gave some good advice to people sitting at home. You took a lot of the mystery out of illness and that usually helps to put people's minds at rest.'

He staggered backwards as though she had stunned him with her praise. 'Am I hearing this right? Did you just say that TV medical shows can make for good viewing?'

Her mouth quirked. 'Sort of. Actually, I thought you were pretty fantastic in front of the cameras. You were so natural, as though they weren't there, and you seem to be able to create an instant rapport with the audience. I'm envious. I don't think I would ever be confident in that situation. You make it look so easy.'

He put a hand to her forehead. 'Are you sure you're quite well? This is not like you at all.'

She batted his hand away with a flick of her fingers. She gave a wry smile. 'Enough… You're the one who ought to be having his brow felt. I don't know what you're doing here when you only managed a few hours' sleep last night, and you must be worried sick about your sister and brother-in-law. I don't know how you manage to fool everyone with that calm manner. I've seen your strained expression when you think no one's looking.'

'Being at work helps me to get through it.' His expression was serious. 'I've asked Kim to ring around the hospitals in the area near to where their boat was lost to see if anyone comes in over the next few days. I'm clinging to the hope that they might still turn up.'

She could feel the torment he was going through. Seeing his rigid features, she wanted to reach out and touch him and let him know that she was there to share his pain. If there was any way she could have taken it on herself, she would have.

Instead, she asked quietly, 'Do you know roughly where the boat went missing?'

He nodded. 'I went out there in a motor launch myself, so that I could follow the coastline and see what kind of territory they were dealing with. Some debris was found a day or so ago, floating up onto the shore. We think the boat was tossed onto rocks, and I wanted to see if they could have made it to dry land. Amy's a good swimmer, and so is Tim, but it depends on whether they were hurt when the boat fell apart. They were both wearing life jackets, according to someone who saw them leave.'

'You must have had a hectic couple of days, trying to pull everything in. I'm not surprised you didn't manage to call me with any news.'

His mouth straightened. 'I tried, but I couldn't get a signal, and then my battery died on me, and in the end I thought I would be back with you soon enough anyway. I would have liked to say hello to Jacob and Sarah, but I knew that they would be all right, and that you would take good care of them.'

She absorbed that, but didn't comment. At least he had tried, even if it hadn't been her he had wanted to speak to. She countered her disappointment about that by telling herself that it was only natural that he would be concerned about his niece and nephew.

He was heading towards the ambulance bay as they spoke, getting ready to receive his incoming patient, and Abby needed to go and find the next patient on her list.

Helen caught up with them as they were about to go their separate ways. 'I made the appointment for you,

Abby,' she said. 'It's for lunchtime today. You hadn't made any plans for then, had you?'

'Um… I thought…'

Helen shook her head. '"Um" is not the right answer. One o'clock. I'll go with you to offer moral support.'

Abby winced. 'There's no need for you to do that.'

Helen wasn't having any of it. 'It's already a done deal. I'll come and find you.'

Matt gave Abby a concerned glance. 'Is something wrong?'

'No,' she said. 'Nothing's wrong.' Except that her world seemed to have been turned upside down of late. She hadn't been able to understand why it mattered so much to her that Matt might have made the effort to talk to her while he'd been away, but it had dawned on her just now with aching certainty.

She had fallen in love with him. Over these last few weeks she had gone full circle in her feelings towards him, and all she wanted now was for him to return her love.

It wasn't going to happen, though, was it? He was self-sufficient, a man who was in control of himself at all times, and he simply didn't need her the way she needed him.

She would have done better to keep her heart intact and do away with any emotional entanglements. They only led to pain and heartache.

CHAPTER NINE

'WOULD you give me a hand here, Sam?' Abby asked, putting her head around the treatment-room door and calling out to him as he was passing by. 'I need you to set up an intravenous line while I finish preparing an infusion.'

'Sure. What are we dealing with?' He came into the room and looked at the young girl who was lying on the bed. He frowned. She was around eight years old, pale and sweaty, and her blood pressure had dropped to a dangerous level.

'I think it's an adder bite. The weather's warming up and the family were out for a walk in the countryside when Angie here felt a nasty sting to her leg.' Abby showed him the two puncture marks and Sam winced.

Looking at the girl, he said, 'How are you feeling, Angie?'

'Awful,' she mumbled. 'I feel faint and dizzy, and there are pins and needles in my legs.'

'The faintness is because your blood pressure is so low. I'm going to give you something that will stop all that, and we'll soon have you on the mend.' He started to prepare the line, and added, 'Did you see what it was that bit you?'

'No. I just saw something slither away into the bracken.'

Abby had finished cleaning the wound and was preparing the antivenin in a saline solution, when Angie said convulsively, 'I'm going to be sick.'

Sam reached for a kidney bowl just in time. 'Phew, that was a close one,' he said. He glanced across the bed at Abby.

'That's why I needed a hand,' she murmured. 'All the nurses are rushed off their feet, and Helen has gone with a patient up to the children's ward. As to Matt, he dashed off to take a phone call just before his shift was due to end, and I'm assuming he must have gone home by now.'

Sam helped Angie to wipe her face and then dispensed with the bowl. 'Better now?' he asked, and she nodded. 'Good. I'll get you a fresh bowl, just in case.'

To Abby, he remarked, 'Helen said she would look in on the four-year-old who fell from a window and fractured his skull. I heard he was getting along all right, but he would be in hospital for a little while longer.'

'That's right. He seems to be doing well.'

Sam set up the infusion of colloid, and Abby added the antivenin. 'We'll give her this slowly, over the course of an hour so that we can avoid any adverse reactions.'

Sam nodded. 'I thought Matt looked a bit grim when he went to take the phone call. It was an international call from Greece, the desk clerk said, so I guess it must be about his sister and her husband. I hope it wasn't more bad news. Did he say anything to you before he left?'

She shook her head. 'No, not a word. I was with a patient and he might have decided not to interrupt.' It was the best interpretation she could put on it, but it hadn't really surprised her that he had gone without saying anything. He might be an extrovert in front of the cameras, but he could be remarkably close-mouthed when it came to his private life. He hadn't even confided in anyone that his sister was missing until she'd been gone for a couple of days.

Abby grimaced. It hurt that he didn't feel able to confide in her.

She was still dwelling on that when her shift finished later that afternoon. A phone call from Greece could potentially be earth-shattering for him, and she so much wanted to share the important things in his life. Would he ever be ready to include her in them?

Back at the cottage she started on her chores, making sure that everything was neat and tidy, but her heart wasn't in it. Her home had always been special to her, a small but cherished haven, yet now it seemed desolate without Matt or the children there.

She started on a baking session, making a batch of fruit tarts, and the aroma of sweet pastry filled the air. It was a comforting kind of smell, and it tweaked her appetite, so that after she had turned her efforts out onto a wire tray she set about preparing a light meal for herself.

The front doorbell rang as she was tossing a salad. Wiping her hands on a towel, she hurried to answer it, and her face lit up in a smile when she saw who was standing there.

'We brought you some flowers,' Jacob said, giving her a shy glance from under his lashes and thrusting a posy of carnations and freesias into her hands.

'They're to say thank you for looking after us,' Sarah added, giving her a beaming smile.

Matt stood behind the children, a hand on each one's shoulder, so that they presented a united group.

'Oh, they're absolutely lovely. Thank you so much.' She bent to hug the children and then stood back to let them scamper into the house. She glanced up at Matt. 'Thank you for that, it was a beautiful thought, but I was glad to be able to help out. I want you to know that I'm here for you any time you need me.'

His mouth curved. 'Now, that is a delightful prospect. Could I have it in writing?'

She grinned at him. 'That depends. Would I get the same kind of commitment from you?'

'Now, that is something to definitely think about,' he said.

They walked into the kitchen where Jacob was eyeing up the food that was laid out on the table. His eyes were wide. 'You have cake,' he said, 'and little fruit pies. I like those. Especially the fruit pies.' He gave her an appealing look. 'I haven't had my tea yet because Uncle Matt said we were coming straight here.'

Sarah dug him in the ribs. 'You're being cheeky,' she said.

'No, I'm not. I'm just saying I like fruit pies.'

'You are, too.'

'Am not.' He glowered at his sister.

'I think,' Abby said, 'that it would be good if you all had tea with me. I was going to have a cheese salad, but there's some ham and chicken in the fridge, so we could have that as well, if you like.'

'Yes, please,' Jacob said. 'Were you going to eat all that cake and all those pies yourself?'

Abby chuckled. 'No, actually, I couldn't make up my mind which of them to have.' She started to lay cutlery out on the table, and Sarah fetched plates from the cupboard and set them out.

'I'll make a pot of tea, shall I?' Matt suggested, and she nodded. Suddenly, life was so much brighter now that he was there.

'I'll sit down at the table and make sure you don't forget anything,' Jacob said, and Abby laughed.

'That sounds like a good idea.' She sent Matt an oblique glance. 'You look as though you're in a good mood,' she murmured. 'I heard about your phone call this morning. Has Kim managed to come up with some news?'

'Better than that,' he said. He brought the teapot over to the table and set it down, adding cups and saucers.

'They've found my mum and dad,' Sarah put in quickly, her mouth breaking into an excited smile.

'How could they find them?' Jacob said, as though his sister didn't have a clue. 'They weren't lost.' He looked at her as though she was slightly dotty, and Abby guessed that he had no idea at all about what had been going on.

Sarah gave her brother a quelling look, but by then he was tucking into cheese and coleslaw and he was oblivious to what was going on around him.

'So they've been found?' Abby said, her eyes bright with wonder. She turned to Matt and he nodded.

'They were picked up from a small uninhabited island this morning.' He sat down and started to help himself to food. 'Apparently they had managed to get themselves to shore after the boat broke up, but they were exhausted and shocked from the cold of the water. They had to find shelter among the trees, and I suppose that's why no one was able to find them.'

'Oh, Matt, that's wonderful news. Have you spoken to them?'

He nodded. 'This afternoon. They sound as though they're well enough, but they were both suffering from exposure and dehydration, so they've been taken to a hospital to recover. They'll probably be staying there for a day or so.'

'How was it that they were found?'

'Tim managed to rig up a flagpole from a tree branch and then he tied his shirt to it in the hope that it would catch the attention of anyone in a passing boat. He wrote SOS in pebbles on the shore. There wasn't much of a shore, apparently, because the island was mostly sheer rock faces, but some sightseers from a nearby island went exploring one day and caught sight of them.'

'Uncle Matt had left some photos and notices with the people on the islands around there,' Sarah put in, 'so we think they were looking to see if anyone was there. Most people thought they wouldn't have been able to climb up the rock sides, but my dad's good at that sort of thing. He helped Mum get up to the top.'

Matt grimaced. 'He said it was either that or be pulled back out to sea by the tide.'

'It was a good thing that you went out there,' Abby said with a relieved smile, 'otherwise the islanders might not have been looking for them for much longer. You must have stirred their interest.' She sent him a curious glance. 'I don't suppose, after all that effort and mayhem, they managed to find a villa?'

Matt smiled and shook his head. 'No, they didn't, and, to be honest, I think they've changed their minds about looking any further.'

'Mum says she doesn't want to look at another property in Greece or the islands—not for a long while anyway.' Sarah put down her fork. 'She said she kept thinking about us and worrying, and she won't be happy until she's back home again, so Uncle Matt is going to take us over there to fetch them.'

'I'm really glad for you,' Abby said. 'This must be the best news ever.'

'Does anyone want that last apple pie?' Jacob put in. 'Because, if you don't, I could eat it up. I've still got room.'

'You always have room,' Sarah declared. 'That's why Dad says you're a bottomless pit.'

Jacob frowned. He didn't understand what his sister was talking about, but after due consideration he must have decided that it didn't matter anyway, and as no one laid claim to it, the pie was his.

'I'm not surprised he likes them so much,' Matt said. 'They're home-made, aren't they?' He glanced at Abby, a dark brow lifting.

Abby nodded. 'I was at a bit of a loose end when I came home from work. I knew you'd had a phone call and it felt a bit strange, not knowing what was happening. I just needed to be busy, so baking seemed like a good idea.'

Matt gave a rueful grimace. 'I wanted to tell you earlier, but you were with a patient and I'd promised I would ring Kim back. I decided to make all the arrangements for going out there to pick them up, and I thought it would be good if I brought the children here with me so that we could tell you when we were all together.'

'It was good. I'm really happy that you came here.'

'Can we go and play in the garden?' Jacob wanted to know. 'I made a den in the shed when we were here before, and I want to see if it's still there.'

'It is,' Abby said. 'I haven't moved anything. Just be careful you don't trip over the lawnmower.'

'I want to play as well,' Sarah cut in. 'I'm going to be the lady who makes the house look nice.'

'And I'm the pirate who brings the jewels back.' Jacob was already following her out of the door.

'It's good to see Sarah looking so happy,' Abby commented, watching them go.

Matt nodded. 'She's been under a tremendous strain lately. She doesn't always show it because she's a quiet girl, but still waters run deep with her and a lot goes on in her head.'

'Yes, I've noticed that.' She stood up and started to clear the table. 'You must be so relieved to know that your sister is safe and well.'

He got to his feet and began to put things away in the fridge. 'I am. These last few days have been a living nightmare, but all this has made me stop and think about life in a different way. Things can change in an instant, and I realise that you need to go for whatever is uppermost in your mind. Grab it while you can, because you never know when you're going to run out of time. I don't want my life to be full of missed opportunities.'

She paused, closed the dishwasher and leant back against the worktop, looking him over thoughtfully. 'Such as? What have you missed out on?'

'A loving relationship and family, perhaps. Not that I would want a family straight away, but I know that Amy and Tim have a good marriage, and having Jacob and Sarah stay with me made me see how much fun there is to be had when the house is full of children. It had never occurred to me before that there was any other kind of existence than the one I'm living now. It makes me wonder what it would be like to lead a different kind of life.'

'Different from being the wayward bachelor who flits from one woman to the next, you mean?'

He laughed. 'Whatever gave you the idea that description had anything to do with me?'

She gave him a quizzical glance. 'Well, there's Amy and Tim, and Jacob and Sarah's take on it for a start.'

He made a wry face. 'You've been listening to the children.'

'Shouldn't I have?'

He came over to her and placed his hands around her rib cage, leaning into her and kissing her softly on the mouth. 'I think,' he murmured, 'that you should take your cue from me.' He kissed her again, and ran his hands over the curve of her hips, easing her against him so that her soft feminine curves melded with his hard, strong body. 'Life is for living, for making the most of what comes our way. You're beautiful, sexy, sweet and caring, and you drive me crazy with wanting you. Did you know that?'

He nuzzled the column of her throat, brushing his lips against the silkiness of her skin. 'You once said you would be here for me whenever I needed you—how can I let that offer pass me by? We could be so good together.'

He kissed her hungrily, and she wound her arms around him, running her fingers over the nape of his neck and letting them tangle with the crisp line of his hair.

He made her long for so much, and all of it had to do with him. He was everything she wanted…his touch, his warmth, the passionate intensity of his kisses. She could lose herself in him and never give a thought to the outside world.

'Do you think you could ever learn to trust in anyone again?' he asked in a roughened tone. 'Enough to share your life with someone else and all that goes along with living together as a couple?'

Abby eased herself back from him and studied his features for a moment or two. There was a far-away look in his eyes, as though he was thinking aloud, and she wondered what he was really saying to her. Was he asking her to live with him? Was he talking about an affair, rather than marriage? Or was he thinking about the prospect of having children at some point in the future?

'I'm not sure what you're asking,' she said, 'and who can say that they know for sure that what they want is within reach? You could live with someone and find that it didn't work out, and as to children, who knows what might happen? There must be a lot of people who long for children and then find that it's not possible to have them.'

He looked at her curiously, his head tilted a little to one side. 'I suppose that's true, but I don't see how that would come into the picture right now…unless…' He held her away from him a fraction and gazed into her eyes. 'Unless you're trying to tell me something… Are you saying that you can't have children? Is that what you mean?'

'I suppose so. I mean, I don't know for sure. It's a very big step to take, isn't it, deciding that you want to share your life with someone, and knowing that things might not turn out the way you want them to? It wouldn't matter if neither of you was particularly bothered about starting a family at some point.'

He cupped her shoulders with his hands. 'Abby, you're talking in riddles. Tell me what's wrong. Is there some reason why you think you might not be able to conceive? Is it because you were attacked?'

She nodded. 'I had to have surgery afterwards, and it left me with scar tissue inside. I had a scan to find out what the possibilities were, but it wasn't good news. The doctor thought there might be problems for me. My Fallopian tubes are blocked, and I'm not sure whether they can be cleared. The doctor said there were no guarantees.'

'That must have come as a terrible shock to you.' He looked into her eyes and she could see the compassion in his expression. 'I'm sorry, Abby. I can see how upsetting that must have been for you. You've always been so good with children. I've seen the way you are with the little ones who come into A and E... You hold them and comfort them, and I guessed that you would like to have one of your own one day. Was I right?'

She nodded. 'Yes, but I just can't be sure that it will ever happen.'

'You shouldn't give up hope. There are surgeons who are skilled in the latest laser techniques, and they could do an exploratory operation and possibly clear any scar tissue by means of a laparoscopy, which means there would be hardly any external evidence that you've had surgery afterwards. There's always the possibility that your problem could be solved. Don't you think you should look into it?'

She pressed her lips together to still their trembling. 'What do I do if there's no successful result? How do I live with the knowledge that it might never be possible for me to have a child, to learn that I'm infertile? I long to hold my child in my arms, and it might never happen. My life would be empty.'

'At least you would have tried. Are you going to live with that cloud hanging over you for evermore?'

'I don't know.' She looked up at him, a sheen of tears blurring her vision. 'I don't have the courage to face up to a future that is childless. I realised that when I looked after Jacob and Sarah. They brightened up my world. They made me long for a family of my own.'

'People do manage to cope without them. They adopt, or they decide to work with children, or they fill their houses with a menagerie of pets. People cope in all sorts of ways.'

But would he be prepared to do that? Abby frowned. Would he compromise his desire for a family by involving himself with someone who couldn't give him what he wanted?

In any case, he wasn't even offering her marriage, was he? There was just this nebulous talk about living with someone and perhaps that was just to allow himself a get-out for when he wanted a change and felt like finding someone else to share an interlude with him.

'Maybe they do.'

'I could look into the question of surgery for you, and find someone who has a good track record with the latest techniques. Would you let me do that for you? Where would be the harm?'

'I don't know.'

He put his arms around her and held her close. 'You're braver than you think, Abby. You mustn't give up. Take your troubles by the horns and face up to them. Isn't that what you do in every other aspect of your life?'

'I'm afraid of what I'll find.'

'But you won't be alone in this, Abby. I'll be there to support you.'

Perhaps he was right. Maybe she ought to deal with this problem once and for all. What was the point in pushing her fears into a box? The lid was bound to come off one day and they would still be there for her to face once more. She might as well get it over with.

'All right,' she said, her voice heavy. 'I'll do it.'

'Good girl. You won't regret it, I promise you. I won't let you down.'

She was sure that he meant what he said, but if it

turned out to be bad news for her, would things ever be the same between them again? He was so determined, and now she wondered about the reason for that. Would he care for her enough to want to be with her if she was infertile? Why had he never mentioned love?

He didn't let her dwell on things for long. At work the next day he stayed on after the end of his shift, and she discovered that he was checking through a list of surgeons. 'There are a number who would be able to do the specific surgery you might need,' he told her, 'but the question is whether they can fit you in right away.'

'It doesn't matter if they can't,' she said.

'It does.' He gave her a direct, hard look. 'I'm not giving you the chance to go back on your decision. We'll get it over and done with and then you'll know what's what.'

Abby made a face. 'You're so bossy.'

'Yes, I am.' He grinned at her. 'Makes a change from you calling all the shots, doesn't it?'

She didn't dignify that with an answer, but left him to get on with his search. Half an hour later he came and found her.

'I've made you an appointment with Mr McNulty. He has a private practice some ten miles from here. He'll see you tomorrow for an assessment, and he can fit you in for surgery if necessary on the weekend.'

Abby's mouth dropped open in surprise. She hadn't really expected him to come up with anything, and certainly not for the appointments to be so soon. 'I don't think—'

'There's no "I don't think" about it,' he said. 'He's an excellent surgeon, one of the best, and I know him personally. He owes me a favour or two, and he's agreed to take you on especially for me. So it's all done and dusted and you can't get out of it.'

Abby was troubled. There he was again, insisting that this be carried through. Was it only for her benefit that he was pushing the issue, or was there something else going on in his mind? Why was this so important to him? Would he still care for her in quite the same way if the surgery turned out to be a failure?

He frowned. 'I have to go over to Greece to fetch Amy and Tim back home on the day of the operation, so I won't be able to be here, but I'll ask Helen if she'll go with you to the clinic. I know you and she get along very well. You need someone to be with you.'

He touched her arm lightly. 'I wish I could stay with you, but I can't let Jacob and Sarah down. I promised them I would take them to their parents.'

'I know. I understand. Besides, Amy has been through an awful lot by the sound of things, and she'll need you to be there with her.'

'Thanks, Abby. I knew you would understand.' He glanced at his watch. 'I'm late. I have to go over to the studios this afternoon—they want me to outline an idea for a TV show to go out at the weekend.'

'I thought you'd finished all your shows for the time being?'

'I have, but this is a one-off. They have a slot to fill because some other show has been cancelled, and they asked if I would step in.'

'Can you come up with something at short notice?'

'Yes, I've an idea for a project. It doesn't take me long to write a script, and then it's just a question of bringing in the specialist people to take part. We'll record it in a couple of days' time before I go off to Greece.'

'That's fast work.'

'Yes, but sometimes it's good to be able to accommodate the producers this way. It shows them that you're professional, and it makes for a good working relationship.'

She guessed she wouldn't be seeing much of him over the next day or so if he was working and fitting everything in around the children. It made her sad, because she wanted to be with him more and more.

It turned out that Helen was a better friend than Abby had ever realised. 'Matt didn't need to ask me to come with you,' she said, when the day for her surgery dawned and they arrived at the clinic. 'I'd have come along anyway.'

She helped Abby to set out her belongings from her overnight bag in her room. 'I'll stay with you while you have the surgery,' she said, 'and I'll be here for you when you come round from the anaesthetic.'

She looked around the room that was to be Abby's during her stay at the private hospital. 'This is quite cosy, isn't it? It's all very tastefully done out.'

Her glance went to the fruit bowl that was piled high with oranges, apples and grapes. 'They're from Matt, aren't they? He said he was going to send some. Of course, I might work my way through all your grapes because I can't resist them, and you probably won't feel like eating anything afterwards, will you?'

'I doubt it. Anyway, you're welcome to help yourself.' It had been thoughtful of Matt to send them. He couldn't be there himself, so he was making sure his presence was there in other ways.

There were also flowers in the room, a beautiful arrangement of roses and love-in-a-mist, and when Abby checked the card that had come with them, she saw that they were from Matt, too.

'I wish I could be there for you,' he'd written, 'but I'll be thinking of you all the time.'

Abby felt a small glow of warmth start up inside her. Maybe the thought that he cared for her enough to do this would carry her through.

The nurse came to take her to Theatre a short time later, and she kept the vision of those flowers locked inside her like a treasure that was to be guarded at all costs.

When the surgery was over, she was wheeled back to her room and Helen waited with her while the effects of the anaesthetic wore off. 'How did it go? Did Mr McNulty say?'

'He didn't say very much at all,' Abby murmured, still drowsy and with her head feeling like a cloud of cotton wool. 'I think he seemed fairly satisfied with the way things went. I said I'd send you out for more information. If it's OK with you, I'd rather hear the news from a friend.'

'I'll see if I can find out any more for you.' Helen was about to scoot off in search of the surgeon when the phone rang. Abby was drifting off into sleep.

'It's Matt,' Helen said, smiling. 'Do you want to speak to him?'

'Yes, please.'

'She's still a bit woozy from the anaesthetic,' Helen said into the receiver. 'She might not make a whole lot of sense just yet.' She handed the phone to Abby and then quietly left the room.

'How are you, Abby? Are you feeling all right?'

'I think so. I'm a bit floaty…sort of drifting on a cloud.'

'That sounds like quite a nice feeling.' He chuckled. 'I wish I could float along with you. Do you know how the operation went? Has the surgeon told you anything yet?'

'I'm not sure. It's all a bit vague, really.'

'He's probably waiting until you've had time to come round properly, and I should do the same. I just wanted to know that you were safe.'

'I am.'

They spoke for a little while longer, and then Matt said, 'I want you to be sure to take care and get plenty of rest. I should be back tomorrow, and I'll come and pick you up from the hospital in the afternoon.'

'I will. Thanks. It's lovely to hear your voice.'

'Me, too. I miss you.'

They ended the call and Abby replaced the phone on its pod as Helen came back into the room.

'Mr McNulty seems to think that everything's all right,' Helen said, looking pleased. 'He says you need to go for a check-up in a couple of months' time, but things are looking good. That's brilliant news, isn't it?'

'It's fantastic.' Abby's voice was muffled with drowsiness and Helen smiled.

'You look as though you could do with some more sleep,' she said. 'Shall I leave you to rest?'

Abby nodded. 'Yes, if you like. It's been so good of you to stay with me for all this time.' Her mouth made a sleepy smile. 'Besides…' she yawned '…you have the chance of a hot date, don't you? Why don't you give Martin a ring and say you'll meet up with him somewhere?'

Helen's cheeks flushed with warm colour. 'How did you know about that? We were being very discreet, I thought.'

Abby blinked in an effort to wake herself up a bit. 'Well, it may have had something to do with the fact that he gets very self-conscious whenever you come into a room. I'll be having a conversation with him when he suddenly loses track of what he's saying and starts giving you surreptitious glances.'

Helen laughed. 'Me, too. I have to concentrate twice as hard when he's around. It must be something in the air.'

'Hmm. Go and meet him.'

Helen didn't need any more telling, and when she had gone Abby settled back against her pillows and dozed for a while. An hour or so later, when the nurse came to check on her, she was awake enough to flick the button on the television's remote control.

A holiday programme was coming to a close. It made her wonder about spending time on a golden beach where the surf would roll gently in, and she found herself daydreaming about Matt being by her side.

And then, all at once, he was there on the screen in front of her, and she realised that this must be the programme he had been talking about, the one that had been slotted in at the last minute.

The introductory credits rolled, and then Matt was standing there, talking persuasively about the problems of women who couldn't have children.

'It's a deeply emotional situation that they find themselves in,' he was saying. 'These women long to hold a child of their own in their arms, but they know that it might never happen and it feels as though their lives are empty.'

Her eyes opened wide to take it all in, and she listened to his words with growing disbelief. He was taking everything she had said and putting it out there on the television for everyone to hear. Thousands of people would be listening in to her distress, knowing about every thought and feeling she'd had.

He didn't mention her by name, of course, and only he and Helen knew that she was here, in this clinic, but it felt as though he was talking about her alone.

'"How do I find the courage to face up to a childless world?" This is what women such as these want to know. What you do,' he said, 'is look for answers.'

He went on to talk about the causes of infertility and how they could be treated. Abby listened, but all the time she felt as though she was being held up for scrutiny. He had taken her medical problem and laid it out for the world to see. This whole programme was an act of betrayal. How could he do this to her? Was nothing sacred?

She had believed that he was sympathetic to her and that he had wanted to help, but now all her illusions were dashed. He had been gleaning material for his own use. She was his research material, his project, and that hurt more than words could say.

CHAPTER TEN

'ARE you sure that you're feeling well enough to leave here on your own?' The nurse was concerned. 'You had an anaesthetic yesterday, and somebody should be with you to make sure that you're all right.'

'I'll be fine,' Abby told her. 'Please, don't worry about me. My temperature and blood pressure were normal when you checked them, and I feel perfectly fit. You were going to let me go home anyway this morning, weren't you, so I'll sign a form to say that I'm discharging myself.'

'Well, at least let me call for a taxi.'

Abby nodded. 'That would be great, thanks.'

While the nurse was doing that, Abby sent a text message for Matt to tell him that she was leaving the clinic and that there was no need for him to come and pick her up. 'Spend some time with your family,' she told him, and then she switched off her mobile so that he wouldn't be able to get in touch.

Her only problem was that he might come over to the cottage to find out what was going on, and she wasn't ready to face up to that just at the moment. The television programme still rankled, and she had to find a way of dealing with all the feelings of hurt and the betrayal that were coursing through her before she came face to face with him once more.

Perhaps a hotel room would be her best option. She had booked a few days off work, so there were no worries on that score. No one would know where to look for her, and she could say that she had been taking a break, getting in a day or so of sunshine and fresh air to help her to recover from the surgery she had undergone.

In truth, she was feeling remarkably fit, and it was only her warring emotions that were letting her down. How could he have done this to her? He was a fink, a snake in the grass, a toad.

'Take me to the Country Park Hotel, would you?' she told the taxi driver. She knew the place from long ago when she had stayed there with friends, celebrating their newly qualified status as doctors. It was a rural retreat, with extended landscaped grounds where she could lose herself in quiet seclusion. More than anything, she needed time to think things through.

'We can offer you a room overlooking the terrace, madam,' the receptionist said brightly, 'or perhaps you would prefer something a little more private? We do have a couple of log cabins situated down by the lake. They're both available as it's early on in the season, so you could take your pick. Of course, they are at least half a mile from the main hotel building, but you could still benefit from the hotel service, and either take your meals in the dining hall or have room service.

And, of course, the conference facilities are available to everyone who stays with us.'

Conference facilities? Abby recalled that business-people often stayed here, hiring the assembly rooms for meetings. There were all the add-ons that came with the territory—telephone, video-conferencing and computer access.

'A cabin sounds wonderful,' Abby said. 'I'll take one of those.'

She spent the next day or so cut off from the outside world. Her meals were delivered to the cabin after a simple phone call, and she would wander down by the lake, breathing in the early summer scents of freshly mown grass or take a walk through the wooded area behind the cabin and feel the soft undergrowth beneath her feet.

All the time she was trying to come to terms with what Matt had done. Wasn't he every bit like her ex, taking what he wanted and using it to his own ends? She had been vulnerable, letting down her guard for the first time in years, and he had used her emotional fra-gility to exploit her. How could she care anything at all for a man like that? Hadn't he destroyed whatever it was that she felt for him?

The truth, though, was that nothing had changed. Deep down she knew that she still loved him. She yearned for him, longed for him to tell her that it was all a mistake. He had not meant to hurt her. He loved her, too.

She wanted to see him, but she wasn't ready to face him yet, so she did the next best thing. Back at the cabin she switched on the laptop computer and accessed his website, touching her finger to the screen where his image appeared.

'This is Matt Calder's website. I hope you tuned in to the TV show this weekend, any of you ladies out there who are worried about the problem of infertility. I wanted to show you that there are all kinds of solutions, but if you missed the show, there's a section here on the website that might be of some help to you.

'Or you could drop me a line with your questions or comments. On that note, we haven't heard recently from that feisty lady, Dr Abby Byford. She has her finger on the pulse of what's going on in the medical world. What do you think, Abby? Did I touch on the right issues? Did the programme go too deep, or not deep enough? Speak to me.'

Abby mulled things over. Was he baffled by her disappearance? Or had he realised what it was that had made her run for cover? Did he know that she had gone away somewhere to lick her wounds?

All in all, she suspected that he knew exactly what was going on. After all, he was astute enough to be able to work things out. He was a thinker, a man who took issues by the throat and dealt with them there and then. He didn't pussyfoot around.

Wasn't that why he had arranged for her to have the surgery, why he had pushed for her to get it done right away? He didn't deal in uncertainties. He simply cleared the path of any debris and moved on to the task in hand.

When his sister had been missing, he'd set out to find her, and he'd put things in motion to continue the search. When Abby had told him about her problem, he had taken action. And then he'd gone on to do what he could for other people.

Had she misjudged him? It was all a question of trust, wasn't it? Perhaps that was the lesson she had yet to learn.

Her fingers strayed to the keyboard. Was she doing the right thing? Not so long ago, everything had seemed pretty clear-cut to her, but now she wasn't so sure.

'I've always wondered,' she wrote, *'why people are so fascinated with watching the difficulties and dilemmas that others go through, but I think I have the answer now. It's because we learn something from them…either what to do, or how to cope, or simply how to comfort others in their distress.*

'My question to you, Dr Calder, would be to ask how you come by your information, and how you decide whether or not to use it. Do you ever feel that you're treading on toes in your efforts to broadcast your message to the world? Isn't it some kind of a betrayal to take the outpourings of emotionally vulnerable women and use them to further your cause?'

Then she hit the button and sent her message into the ether. Let him do with it what he would.

Abby was feeling stronger with every day that passed. As she opened her eyes to each new dawn, she wondered what the future would bring. Out by the lake, she practised skimming pebbles over the water, something her father had taught her to do as a child.

She smiled. Her parents lived some distance away, and she hadn't seen them in a while. Perhaps she would go and visit when she took her next summer break. In the meantime, she would give them a phone call and catch up on the goings on in their neighbourhood.

By early afternoon she was thinking about making her way back to the cabin. Would Matt have posted a reply? He would have finished his work at the hospital by now, and perhaps he would be ready to access his website.

Only as she stared about her, shielding her eyes from the sun, a tall figure came and blocked her view. She saw long legs encased in dark chinos and a shirt that was crisp and fresh and open at the neck. She had to tilt her head back to see his face, but even with the glare of the sunlight behind him casting shadows over his face she knew that it was Matt.

'Hello, Abby.'

He came and sat down beside her and she stared at him in open-mouthed astonishment. 'Matt? How did you know where to find me?'

'It took a bit of working out, but you weren't at the cottage, and you weren't answering your phone, so I guessed that you had gone to ground somewhere. When you sent a message to the website I guessed you had access to a computer from somewhere, but I still couldn't figure it out. I went back to the clinic, and the nurse told me you left by taxi, so the next thing was to contact the taxi firm and find out where they had taken you.'

He made a wry face. 'I did use a bit of subterfuge at that stage, because I said you'd had surgery and we were concerned for your well-being.'

'As you can see, I'm fine.'

'Yes. You look good.' His gaze moved over her. 'I was worried about you, though, and I missed you. I couldn't understand why you didn't wait for me to come and bring you home from the clinic…until I saw what you wrote on the website.'

'And now?'

'And now I'm not entirely sure.' He reached for her hand and enclosed it within his. 'I think you felt that I used you as some kind of pawn in my own game, but it wasn't like that. I hoped you would know me better than to think I was capable of something like that.'

She smiled at him. 'I've come to realise that myself. I think I just needed to hear you say it.'

He tilted his head on one side and looked at her. 'I'm not like your ex-boyfriend, Abby. I'm not devious, or grasping, or wanting things for my own ends. I'm a doctor because I care about people and I want to do the best for them. What you said to me about not being able to have children, about the sense of loss and the unbearable feelings that it causes…you're not the only one to have that emotional uncertainty. I've heard it so many times in my role as a doctor. I've even heard it from my own sister.'

She stared at him. 'From Amy?'

'Yes. She used to suffer from endometriosis until she had treatment. She thought she wouldn't be able to conceive, and it was a terrible time for her and for all of us who cared about her.'

'I overreacted,' she said. 'I can see that now, but I needed this time alone so that I could work things out for myself.'

'I wish you had confided in me.' He put his arms around her and held her to him. 'I can't bear the thought of you going off on your own and suffering this way. We should be able to work things out together. Always.'

'Always? You didn't feel able to tell me what was going on when you first heard that your sister was missing. I felt as though I was pushed out, as though you didn't want to share your troubles with me.'

'That's because I wasn't sure what was going on. I didn't want to worry you. I should have told you, I realise that now. From now on we'll talk things through and work out our problems together.'

'Will we?'

'We will, I promise you.'

She looked up into his blue eyes and saw the sun reflected there. His gaze promised hope and contentment and infinite togetherness.

'I love you, Abby. I want to be with you for ever and a day. You don't ever need to doubt me, because you're everything I could ever want.'

Her heart leapt at what he was saying. More than anything she wanted to believe him, but would he feel the same way if he was to discover that her surgery had been a failure? Had his motivation been entirely for her well-being, or had part of it been to do with the fact that he, too, wanted to have children of his own one day? Somehow she couldn't quite find the words to question him about that.

Instead, she murmured, 'Are you quite sure?' She plucked at a blade of grass, and then looked up at him once more. 'Only there were these rumours—about you never wanting to settle down, that you were having too much fun as a single man.'

He laughed. 'I shall have to have words with my family on that score. They think because I'm on TV and I get all this fan mail that I actually enjoy the attention and have my pick of whoever is out there.'

He shook his head. 'Nothing could be further from the truth, in fact. I learnt a long while ago that people identify with me on TV. I got into it by chance because the press came along when I was helping an accident victim and I answered their questions and helped everyone to make sense of what was going on. It was a kind of overnight fame and I thought it was a flash in the pan, but it turned out that it wasn't.'

'So you don't crave the single life?'

'I don't. Especially not now. Ever since I first met you I've been intrigued by you, Abby. I think about you all the time and I want to be with you.' He hesitated. 'That's why I thought perhaps we could be married. Only you didn't seem so keen on the idea.'

She looked at him in surprise, and also in wonder. 'I don't recall that you ever mentioned marriage. You said something about living together.'

'No, that's not what I meant at all. I want to make this a true commitment, a statement to the world that you and I are going to be together for ever.'

'And if there are no children?'

He sucked in a breath. 'Oh, Abby, is it true? I'm so sorry.' He pulled her up against him, hugging her tightly as though he would never let her go. 'I asked Mr McNulty about the surgery but he wouldn't tell me anything. Patient confidentiality, he said. I'm so, so sorry.'

She looked at him and saw the compassion in his eyes. 'I know that children are important to you,' she said huskily.

'Yes… But I suppose…I imagine we can find a way around that. And there'll always be Jacob and Sarah to take on outings, or there will be family barbecues where we can all have fun together. It won't be so bad.'

'Won't it?'

'No. We'll make it work somehow, even if we have to borrow a couple of kids.' He chuckled, and she thumped his arm playfully.

'I'm being serious about this.'

He sobered. 'I know. It's a blow, but it's not the end of the world and we'll sort something out. We might even be able to try IVF.'

She was silent, and he tilted her chin so that she was looking up at him. 'I love you, Abby,' he said, planting a kiss on her lips, 'and I want to marry you. Will you have me?'

'Oh, yes, please,' she murmured, and kissed him back. The kiss went on for quite some time, and when they finally came up for breath she said in a roughened voice, 'Oh, by the way, about the surgery…it was actually a success. Mr McNulty said I shouldn't have any problems from now on. They tested the patency of the Fallopian tubes before they brought me round, and everything was fine. I have to have a check-up in a couple of months, but he doesn't foresee any problems.'

His mouth dropped open in surprise. 'You were kidding me? You let me think that it wasn't possible.'

He gave a ragged laugh. 'You little witch, I'm going to kiss you senseless for that. Just you see...'

It was a long, long while after that before either of them wanted to see the light of day once more, but eventually Abby snuggled into the crook of his arm and they both looked out over the gently rippling water of the lake.

'Did you post a reply on your website?' she asked.

He nodded. 'I said more or less what I said to you, that many women feel the same way about this issue of fertility and that the comments don't come from anyone in particular.'

'Hmm. You called me a feisty lady.'

He gave a rueful smile. 'It's what you are. I noticed that right from the first. You don't give up no matter what, you say what you think, and above all you face up to what life throws at you. The only difference now is that we'll face up to it together.'

She turned to hug him close. 'I love you,' she said softly. 'I don't think I've told you that before, have I?'

He gently nuzzled her throat. 'No, you haven't. Do you want to tell me again?'

'I do. I definitely do.' She wound her arms around him, and kissed him soundly on the mouth. He wound his arms even more firmly around her, his hands caressing her soft curves and turning her blood to flame, making her body tremble with need. Neither of them surfaced until much, much later. And in the following month, people who wanted to contact Matt via the Internet found a message that read:

'Welcome to Matt Calder's website. For those of you looking for my daily diary, I'm afraid I'll not be

with you for the next few weeks. Instead, I'll be walking down the aisle of my local church with my wonderful bride, Abby. Then, after a lovely reception with family and friends, we'll be setting off for a blissful honeymoon, somewhere exotic, where the surf rolls in over golden beaches and we can sip pina coladas until the sun goes down.

'But I promise...I'll be back....'

MILLS & BOON

MEDICAL

Proudly presents

Brides of Penhally Bay

*A pulse-raising collection of emotional,
tempting romances and heart-warming stories by
bestselling Mills & Boon Medical™ authors.*

January 2008
The Italian's New-Year Marriage Wish
by Sarah Morgan

Enjoy some much-needed winter warmth with
gorgeous Italian doctor Marcus Avanti.

February 2008
The Doctor's Bride By Sunrise
by Josie Metcalfe

Then join Adam and Maggie on a 24-hour rescue mission
where romance begins to blossom as the sun starts to set.

March 2008
The Surgeon's Fatherhood Surprise
by Jennifer Taylor

Single dad Jack Tremayne finds a mother for his
little boy – and a bride for himself.

*Let us whisk you away to an idyllic Cornish town –
a place where hearts are made whole*

COLLECT ALL 12 BOOKS!

Available at WHSmith, Tesco, ASDA, and all good bookshops
www.millsandboon.co.uk

Celebrate 100 years of pure reading pleasure with Mills & Boon®

To mark our centenary, each month we're
publishing a special 100th Birthday Edition.
These celebratory editions are packed with extra
features and include a FREE bonus story.

Now that's worth celebrating!

4th January 2008

The Vanishing Viscountess by Diane Gaston
With FREE story The Mysterious Miss M
*This award-winning tale of the Regency Underworld
launched Diane Gaston's writing career.*

1st February 2008

Cattle Rancher, Secret Son by Margaret Way
With FREE story His Heiress Wife
Margaret Way excels at rugged Outback heroes...

15th February 2008

Raintree: Inferno by Linda Howard
With FREE story Loving Evangeline
*A double dose of Linda Howard's heady mix of
passion and adventure.*

Don't miss out! From February you'll have the
chance to enter our fabulous monthly prize draw.
See special 100th Birthday Editions for details.

www.millsandboon.co.uk

4 FREE

BOOKS AND A SURPRISE GIFT!

We would like to take this opportunity to thank you for reading this Mills & Boon® book by offering you the chance to take FOUR more specially selected titles from the Medical™ series absolutely FREE! We're also making this offer to introduce you to the benefits of the Mills & Boon® Reader Service™—

- ★ FREE home delivery
- ★ FREE gifts and competitions
- ★ FREE monthly Newsletter
- ★ Exclusive Reader Service offers
- ★ Books available before they're in the shops

Accepting these FREE books and gift places you under no obligation to buy, you may cancel at any time, even after receiving your free shipment. Simply complete your details below and return the entire page to the address below. You don't even need a stamp!

YES! Please send me 4 free Medical books and a surprise gift. I understand that unless you hear from me, I will receive 6 superb new titles every month for just £2.89 each, postage and packing free. I am under no obligation to purchase any books and may cancel my subscription at any time. The free books and gift will be mine to keep in any case.

M8ZED

Ms/Mrs/Miss/Mr ....Initials ....
BLOCK CAPITALS PLEASE

Surname ....

Address ....

....

....Postcode...................................

Send this whole page to:
UK: FREEPOST CN81, Croydon, CR9 3WZ